the foreve
book (

when forever comes

TAWNI SUCHY

To the girls who think all the 'good ones' are taken, God's design for your life is beyond your wildest imagination. His plan for you is personal and His timing is perfect.

CONTENTS

Endorsements

"Tawni Suchy weaves together a sweet and endearing second chance romance in this heart—warming novella. Filled with swoony moments, a little mystery, faith elements, and sweet gestures, *When Forever Comes* shows us that even when our lives seem to be falling apart, God is faithful to work all things together for His purposes and our good."

- Latisha Sexton, author of *Never Ending Mercy*

"Tawni delivers a heaping dose of swoon without the spice in this sweet billionaire romance! With a memorable cast of characters, a lush, tropical setting, and a slow-burn second-chance love story that weaves themes of grace and forgiveness throughout, this was easily the best novella I've picked up this year!"

- Dulcie Dameron, author of *The River Hollow Romance Series*

"If you enjoy a strong hero that knows exactly what he wants and doesn't hesitate to grab it, When Forever Comes is the swoony, refreshing, intriguing tale of second chance love that will thrill you. Don't miss out on this story of betrayal, true love, comeuppance, and adventure."

- Hannah Hood Lucero, author of *Cathey's Creek Road*

Synopsis

A decade of prayers reunited them.
Only a miracle can keep them together.

Olivia Swann

Taking my sister on my honeymoon was never part of the plan. But neither was finding my now ex-best friend and fiancé in bed together the day before our wedding. Instead of dwelling on my failed relationship, my sister and I embarked on the vacation of a lifetime. I was ready to enjoy the exclusive resort and all it had to offer. What I wasn't prepared for was running into the boy—now man—of my past, who vanished after giving me the kiss of a lifetime.

Weston Lockwood

It broke me to abandon the only girl I ever loved. But when my careless actions brought tragedy to our hometown, the only option was to leave her behind. Ten years have passed and in that time, I've built my empire, but Olivia never strayed far from my thoughts or prayers. When I found out she was engaged to my high school nemesis, I thought a second chance would be impossible. But when she showed up at my resort on her honeymoon without her fiancé, I knew this was God giving me the second chance I've been praying for.

Will Olivia and West claim their happily ever after? Or will hurts from past wounds destroy their chance at forever?

Delight yourself in the LORD, and he will give you the desires of your heart.

Psalm 37:4

ONE

Olivia

I can't believe I let Dana talk me into this. One day after my almost wedding, and I'm on a private jet with my sister heading to what was supposed to be my honeymoon.

Brad went overboard when he booked this crazy-expensive resort. But when I found out—at the airport—that he had also booked the resort owner's private plane as part of our honeymoon package, I was even more surprised at his over-the-top plans. Although I shouldn't have been. Brad has always been obsessed with status.

Dana was supposed to cancel our reservation since Brad refused to help with any of the wedding-related cancella-tions. After she called and they informed her the trip was non-refundable, she convinced me to keep the reservation and go on my honeymoon with her... on Brad's dime.

"He owes you this much," she had said.

The moment I stepped onto this plane, I felt like I was walking into the living room in a beautiful home. Instead of rows of seats, two sofas face each other with a coffee table settled between them. Toward the back sits a dining room table for four with a beautiful flower arrangement placed at the center.

The deep blue ceiling, with a spattering of white twinkling lights, looks like the night sky. Hardwood flooring spans the full interior and it looks as if it's been freshly polished.

The only other people on board are the flight attendant and the two pilots.

I feel slightly guilty that we're taking advantage of Brad's extravagance without him. But Dana is right. I deserve some compensation for his betrayal.

I spent the last five years dedicated to him and he thanked me by cheating on me the day before our wedding. So, yes, he owes me this.

I'm just grateful I learned about his wandering ways before we got married. Better to learn about them now than after I take his name.

"Liv!" Dana waves her hands in front of my face and points to the flight attendant. I blink my vision into focus and give the woman my attention.

"What can I get you to drink?" she asks.

"Ginger ale, no ice, please."

She disappears behind a curtain at the back of the plane.

When she returns, she's pushing a cart with two silver plates stacked high with delicious looking food and the drinks Dana and I asked for.

"Do you need anything else?" she asks.

After glancing over at Dana and confirming she needs nothing more, I say, "I think we're good. Thank you."

"Enjoy your meal." She disappears behind the curtain again.

Guilt starts nipping at my conscience again as I stare at the platter. My guilt fades away as my hunger deepens.

Dana mumbles, "He really outdid himself." I think she's talking about Brad, but she's never been his biggest fan, and I doubt she'd give him credit for anything positive. Before I can ask her what she means, she shoves an apricot jam cracker in my mouth and all thoughts outside of this delectable food leave me.

I eat to contentment, then lean back and get comfortable.

"This is the life." Dana kicks off her shoes and slides her legs onto the couch, I presume to take a nap.

I narrow my eyes at her. "It's the life, all right. But not yours or mine," I say.

"It could be," she responds, sitting up. "Finish writing some books, publish them, snag a few movie deals, and boom, you'd be a millionaire."

"Easier said than done." I huff and cross my arms over my chest. "I'd need to finish a decent manuscript first."

"Why don't you finish one, then?" Dana asks, as if it's the easiest thing in the world.

I've always wanted to be an author. Not for fame or fortune, but to be the crafter of happily ever afters. To create a story with the twenty-six letters of the alphabet where it all works out in the end has been the dream of my heart since I was a little girl.

In every one of my books, I have the heartbreak down. The breakups are solid. The hurt is palpable. But for the life of me, I can't write the scenes where the characters find the light after their dark moments. Now that my heart is battered, I don't know if I will ever have the skill to give my characters the happy ending they've fought for.

"Have you ever written a book?" I snap.

She lays back down and ignores me, as if she knows she doesn't have a leg to stand on in this discussion. It's a silly thing to get worked up over. I still work at the bank, so it's not like I'm a starving artist. My steady income doesn't give me near the satisfaction a completed manuscript would. Let alone how amazing it would feel to see my books on a book-store shelf.

Neither of us speaks for several minutes. Dana lies on the couch looking as if she doesn't have a care in the world. I envy her. She will be able to enjoy this vacation without the tainted reality I have to face. A reality where the future I had planned is shattered into tiny shards of glass. Where I wasn't enough for the man who promised me forever.

Just like before.

Tears blur my vision. "I should be at home, in front of the TV, watching a sad movie with a bucket of ice cream. Not going on what was supposed to be my honeymoon with my sister."

"Are you saying you don't want to spend this week at the most exclusive resort in the world where you'll be pampered and doted on day and night just because you'll be with me instead of your loser ex?"

Her blunt words cut straight through my walls. I don't respond.

"You need this. Plus, you never know. Maybe you'll find your soul mate while we're there."

I scoff. "You believe in soul mates? Because I don't."

Dana sits up. "I think there's someone out there for everyone. The person God created for you."

"Sounds a little far-fetched." Sure, I write about soul mates in my books, but that's all they are — fiction.

"Okay, forget about the soul mate comment. It's time for you to enjoy your life. You've been so caught up with Brad that you didn't even have fun in college. Now it's time to meet someone new, embrace life, and see where the Brad-free part of your life takes you."

I hold up my pointer finger. "First, college was meant to prepare me for my future. Not teach me how to have fun. Second, I am not ready to move on to someone new. It's all too fresh."

She reaches out and grasps my hand. "Livvy, you never know what the future holds. Don't give up your second chance at love because that idiot cheated. I've told you for years that you can do better."

"Clearly, he got better with Lexi. She's built like a super-model and I'm a chu—"

"Stop!" my sister interrupts me. "Don't even go there. You are gorgeous just as you are. Women envy your curves."

I pull my hand free from hers. "Maybe some of my curves. But not all of them. And I got them all." Brad never failed to point out those imperfections. A huge red flag I ignored time and time again.

Dana rolls her eyes. "That's not even close to being true. Besides, your looks aren't what's most important. It's your beautiful heart. The right guy will see your heart, he'll see your worth, and he'll realize your physical beauty is just the icing on top of the cake."

"Then why wasn't my beautiful heart enough for Brad?"

"Honestly"— she grips my hand again — "he knew you were too good for him."

"Lexi was enough for him." It's not a question, but my sister still has a response.

"Lexi was an easy target. He got what he wanted from her because you wanted to wait."

"Maybe you're right," I whisper before removing my hand from hers and taking a sip of my ginger ale. "Why couldn't he wait just a day longer?" The words are out before I can stop them. It's a question I already know the answer to. Lexi wasn't the first. And if I'm being painfully honest with myself, she wouldn't have been the last.

Brad never was a fan of me waiting until our wedding night for intimacy. But it was a vow I made between me and God, and one I've never regretted making.

Sure, seeing my ex-best friend and almost husband in bed together took me right to the edge of regret. But then I took a step back and can now see it for what it is: a blessing. God's way of throwing me a worn-out lifeline.

It's been less than twenty-four hours since we were supposed to get married. But my path has never been so clear. This was God's final attempt at getting me to walk away from a man He never wanted for me. I could kick myself for straying from God's path for so long.

There's only been one man in my life who I felt God pull me toward. If soul mates are real, he was mine. But after he vanished without a goodbye, I took it as proof that soul mates are a thing found only in fairytales.

He was the first boy I ever loved. And the first boy to break my heart.

I drink the rest of the ginger ale and pull out the book I picked up at an indie bookstore, needing to escape into a fictional world. Just because I can't finish writing a great love story doesn't mean I can't read them.

Amber Island is a four-hour flight from Emerald Springs, the island where we grew up and still live. It gives me plenty of time to get lost in this fictional world of romance and intrigue. I read while Dana naps. I have never been able to sleep while traveling, even as a kid. My sister, however, could fall asleep on a train in the middle of a thunderstorm.

The flight attendant takes our plates and I whisper a thank you so I don't disturb my sister.

By the time I'm halfway through the book, the pilot comes over the intercom and announces our descent, pulling me out of the romantic thriller and waking up my sister.

Dana sits up and rubs her eyes as the pilot says, "I would like to welcome you to Amber Island."

Our personal chauffeur pulls the limousine to the base of the airplane's stairs where I only need to take two steps to get in. It's a short ride, but the service still provides a snack, beverage, and warm compress to unwind from the flight. This place doesn't do mediocre.

"Brad is going to be so mad when he discovers he's paying for our getaway," I say, staring out the window as the palm trees whiz by.

"He deserves to," Dana singsongs. Her feet pound on the floor, sending vibrations up my leg. I assume she's doing her happy dance.

The driver pulls down the road leading to the resort. As I stare out at the gorgeous landscape, guilt eats away at me.

"This was a terrible idea." I cover my face with my hands. "I'm going to pay him back when we get home."

Dana shakes my shoulders. "Oh no, you won't!" She forces me to look at her. "He owes you this. You agreed with me on the plane, remember?"

Before I can answer or object, the chauffeur opens the door and helps Dana and me out.

"I can't wait to see the suite." My sister grabs my hand and squeezes.

We approach the check-in desk where the concierge waits with a smile.

"Welcome to the Golden Sands, how can I help you today?"

"We are here to check in," Dana says.

"Name?" The concierge, whose name tag reads 'Mindy,' asks.

Dana drops her voice to a conspiratorial whisper. "It was under Brad Washburn, but it should be under Olivia Swann now."

Mindy types in the information, and immediately her face falls.

"I am so sorry, but your room was double booked. The other couple is already checked in."

"What?!" Dana exclaims.

I put my hand on my sister's arm to calm her down.

"I am so sorry," Mindy says. "This has never happened before."

"Do you have any other rooms available?" my sister asks.

I already know the answer. This resort is known for its long waitlist. Part of what makes it so exclusive is the difficulty in snagging a reservation. There is no way they have anything available.

The woman gives us a sympathetic smile. "We're fully booked."

It's not surprising. We had to book this place two years in advance. Brad was determined to stay at this resort for whatever reason and made the reservation minutes after he proposed. It was the earliest slot we could get and the reason for our two-year engagement.

The reality of my situation releases the dam of tears I've bottled up since catching Brad and Lexi in the act.

I turn and run to the lobby bathroom, my insides twisting and churning as if they're attempting to dissolve those painful memories. I wallow in self-pity for a few minutes before I hear the gentle squeal of the door opening and closing.

"Liv?" Dana whispers.

I don't answer.

"Livvy, I know you're in here. I'm so sorry. I'm sure it will all work out. It's not like we'll be staying on the streets."

I open the door to the stall I've taken refuge in. "Why can't we just go home?"

"Because I am determined to show you that Brad isn't worth another tear. We are going to have fun. You are going to heal from this."

I pinch the bridge of my nose. "I just want some ice cream."

"They have ice cream here."

"Dana," I warn her, attempting to give her my most intimidating glare.

It fails.

Her expression softens. "We're going to figure this out. I promise." She reaches her hand out and I take it before she pulls me in and hugs me.

Before leaving the bathroom, I remove all traces of my tears and re-apply a swipe of mascara to each eye.

"Gorgeous," my sister says with a wink.

I link my arm with hers, and we head back to the front desk.

When the check-in desk comes into view, however, the young woman is no longer the one standing behind the computer. It's a man who I'm ninety-nine percent sure defined the term "tall, dark, and handsome." His eyes are on the computer screen, a very quizzical look on his chiseled face.

When he lifts his head, he pushes his glasses up the bridge of his nose. "Miss Swann, you asked for me?"

I glance at my sister, who has the largest smirk of her life plastered across her face.

"I asked for the manager. That's you?" Dana asks him.

He nods.

I turn on my sister. "Dana, you asked for the manager? It wasn't that poor woman's fault."

The manager turns his attention to me, and it's like a spark straight to my chest. Something flashes in his eyes but it's gone before I can read it. There is something so familiar about him, but it's as if my heart is blocking my brain from remembering. It's the strangest feeling.

"Yes, I'm W, the manager." He pauses for an awkward second, looking at me as if he's expecting me to do or say something. "After some rearranging, I was able to find you a room."

I want to ask about his odd name, but think better of it.

"You're a lifesaver!" Dana announces, bringing W's focus back to her. "My sister almost had a nervous breakdown when we lost our room. You wouldn't believe the week she's had."

"Oh?" W directs the question at me.

Dana leans forward and plants her hands on the desk and drops her voice to a conspiratorial whisper. "Her fiancé cheated on her with her best friend the night before their wedding. Can you believe that?"

His expression darkens.

I glare at my sister for divulging such a private and delicate piece of information with a stranger, but before I can say a word to her, W says, "No," with full conviction. "Any man who cheats is not worthy of you, Olivia. I'm really sorry you had to go through that." The sincerity of his apology is not lost on me. I don't understand why he seems to care so much.

"Thank you."

Dana stands up straight.

I ask, "How do you know my name?"

"Lucky guess." W shrugs nonchalantly.

I narrow my eyes at him and he smirks, as if he's hiding a fun secret.

"Your name is on the reservation. I heard you call her Dana, which left Olivia."

"What a clever boy," Dana says, and sends him an uncharacteristic wink.

"I aim to please." W's words are directed at me and I can't fight the blush burning my cheeks. When he steps out from behind the desk and motions for us to follow him, his cologne invades my senses and ignites a memory that's just out of reach.

TWO

Olivia

The manager loads our luggage on a cart and leads us to the elevators.

Despite being dressed in an expensive suit, he takes on the job as our bell boy. Maybe he wants to overcompensate for his resort's mess-up.

We follow him to a sleek silver door and he swipes a card over the reader. It beeps and allows us entry.

"Where exactly is this room?" Dana asks as we walk down a mirrored hallway. Motion sensor lights illuminate our path.

"I may have pulled some strings to make up for your misfortune." From the reflection in the mirrored hallway, I see that his once expressive face is now impassive.

W halts and presses his hand against one of the mirrors. A white light scans his hand and the wall opens into an elevator.

Dana leans over and whispers, "Is it just me or do you feel like we're being lured into a supervillain's lair?"

I bite the inside of my cheek to keep myself from laughing.

"After you." W motions for me and my sister to enter and doesn't hide his smile. Dana never has been a good whisperer.

He pushes our luggage in and then presses the button marked PH.

"Wait. There has to be a mistake," I say.

"No mistake, Miss Swann."

"This is the penthouse."

"That's correct. You will be in the penthouse for the duration of your time here. I want to make sure your accommodations match the quality of my—this resort."

I catch my sister's stunned expression in the glass as W tells us about the amenities that will be available to us: a jacuzzi, private infinity pool with a gorgeous view, three bathrooms with a large array of soaps and shampoos, and a butler on demand who will do anything from shining our shoes to tucking us in at night.

The doors open to the most lavish entryway I've ever seen.

A crystal chandelier hangs from the vaulted ceiling. A sweeping staircase off to the left leads up to the loft. Straight ahead is the living room, surrounded by tinted windows showcasing a gorgeous view of the beach.

"This is way too much," Dana says as she steps out of the elevator.

I go over to the windows and look out, but take a few steps back after suddenly realizing I'm in a fishbowl.

W must sense my unease because he says, "It's mirrored glass, so no one can see in. It may not look private, but I can assure you it is."

I eye the people below warily and make a mental note to check the validity of his statement later.

"Why go to all this trouble for us?" I ask, feeling over-whelmed at this generosity.

He stares at me for a long second. No one has looked at me this intensely since high school. I can't look away.

"It's no trouble at all."

"Are you kidding me?" Dana interjects. "This place is the definition of boujie."

W smirks and despite his heavy scruff, the dimple on his left cheek peeks out and reminds me of a certain boy I used to know.

"We can't afford this upgrade!" I can't contain the distress that's evident in my voice. As much as I like the idea of sticking it to Brad, this is too much.

"You don't need to worry about that. This is our way of apologizing for the mix-up," he says.

I want to protest more, but W has made up his mind. His expression leaves no room for argument. "We really appreciate it," I say.

"We do," Dana agrees, then wanders over to the windows.

W watches her for a moment before he turns his attention to me. All thoughts leave my brain. Ocean blue eyes behind rimless glasses hold me captive.

From the corner of my eye, I can see Dana's back is turned to us, and that she's oblivious to our stare down.

Part of me is grateful she's distracted, but another part of me wishes she would see it, so I don't convince myself later that my imagination fabricated it. Something about W is familiar, but there's no way I met him before, right? To forget a face like that would be a travesty.

He takes a step toward me. It looks like he's about to say something, but my question comes out first. "Do I know you?"

My question makes my sister spin on her heel so fast she wobbles on her feet, but she quickly regains her balance.

For some reason, W's face falls. "No. I don't think so." He walks to the elevator. "If there is nothing else, I will let you get back to your vacation." Before leaving, he turns to Dana, not sparing me another glance. "If there is anything you need, phone the concierge and they will get it for you. Thank you for choosing The Golden Shores." He steps onto the elevator, pulling the luggage cart with him, and vanishes behind the doors.

"Where in the world did you hear that pickup line?" Dana asks. "That was seriously worse than 'I lost my phone number. Can I have yours?'" She says the line in an obnoxiously deep masculine voice.

"Doesn't he look familiar to you?"

"Yeah, from my dreams! He's like six foot four and chiseled to the bone!"

I hold back a laugh. "Chiseled to the bone? What does that even mean?"

She releases an exasperated huff. "It means he's built like a bodybuilder. And not like the kind on steroids, but the all-natural ones."

"He was wearing a suit."

She deadpans, "You mean you couldn't make out the flex of those muscles when he unloaded our cart?"

"I wasn't ogling him. Unlike you."

Her mouth drops open, and she places a hand over her chest in mock offense. "How dare you! I wasn't ogling him…" She smirks. "I was admiring him."

"Same thing, in this case."

"W," I test his name—or more accurately, letter—on my tongue. "What does W stand for? No one is just named a letter."

"It's not the most common way to name a baby, but there are other people on the planet with only a letter for a name. It's also a direction on a compass. Maybe that's what you're thinking of."

"No." I'm convinced I know him. There's something overtly obvious that's on the edge of my brain, just out of reach.

"Whatever, since he works here I'm sure you'll have an opportunity to ask him about it." Dana winks before picking up her suitcase and hauling it into the closest bedroom.

I grab mine and choose the other bedroom, located just down the hall. It's all gray, black, and chic. It even smells masculine, like cologne, not a cleaning product or air freshener. It's a familiar scent, too.

I drop my bag on the California King bed's charcoal gray duvet. The bed faces the large picture window, revealing another slice of the beach. The pillows are fluffed and propped against the silver headboard. A Bible rests on the nightstand, but it doesn't look like a hotel Bible. Not with the worn binding and multiple bookmarks. Suddenly I feel like I'm in someone else's home and not a hotel room.

"Hey! Come out here!" my sister calls from somewhere else in the penthouse.

I follow the sound of her voice and end up in the massive kitchen.

"We're in someone else's penthouse." She opens a cupboard, its shelves full of various protein powders and supplements. "No resort or hotel room keeps these stocked. And look at this." She opens another cupboard, revealing canned vegetables.

"Who did he kick out to give us this room?" I ask.

"I dunno..."

I stomp my way back to the bedroom and pick up the Bible from the nightstand. My Bible houses some of my most intimate prayers and pleas, so I do my best to respect the owner's privacy, and keep it closed, not checking to see if there is a name inside. After tucking it safely under my arm, I march my way to the elevator and step in the moment the doors open.

"Where are you going?" my sister asks, sounding panicked.

"I'm not staying in someone else's home."

I punch the L button for Lobby.

"But W said—"

I cut her off. "W is exactly who I plan on confronting."

With that, the doors close and I descend to the bottom floor.

THREE

Olivia

The doors open once I reach the correct floor. My head is down watching my feet move across the marble floor as I work through my thoughts. After two quick strides, I slam into a wall of muscle.

My cheeks heat at my snafu. I look up and open my mouth to apologize to the stranger, but snap it closed when I see who it is.

"Olivia." He makes my name sound like a plea.

"W," I say curtly, straightening my spine. "Just the man I was coming to see."

He rubs the scruff on his face and smiles. "Funny, I was heading up to the penthouse to apologize for my abrupt departure."

I take a couple of steps back and narrow my eyes. "Really?"

He dips his chin. "Yes."

"I'm not the one you should apologize to."

He has the gall to look confused.

"If it's not you and your sister I should apologize to… then who?"

"The person you removed to give us a place to stay just so we wouldn't leave your resort a bad review."

"I didn't remove anyone." He looks to the side, almost as if he's deciding if he should say his next words. "That's where I live. That's my home."

"What? Why would you give up your place for two strangers?"

He licks his lips. "You don't remember me at all, do you?"

"So I *do* know you!" I exclaim, lifting the Bible and shaking it.

W's eyes widen before he snatches the book from my hand and tucks it under an arm. The shock in his eyes is replaced with something new, yet not unfamiliar. It's then that it hits me.

"West. Full name Weston Lockwood, best drum major Emerald High ever had and—"

He interrupts me. "Invisible to the world."

"You know you weren't invisible to me," I say, my heart fluttering at the admission. My fingers itch to touch the stubble on his chiseled jaw to see if it's as soft as it looks. The last time I saw him, West barely had peach fuzz. He looks so different with his rugged scruff than he did as a teenager.

"I know," he states.

We stare at each other for a long moment before he closes the small distance between us. He looks down at me and the emotion in his eyes makes my knees weak.

"You vanished our senior year." I leave the part out about how the last time I saw him, he had me pinned against my locker and kissed me with reckless abandon, not caring who saw his bold act of passion. I was teased about that kiss for the rest of the year, yet I never felt embarrassed.

"So you remember me?" he asks.

"You made a lasting impression on your last day." I raise an eyebrow.

His lips tip up at that. "That was the goal. I hoped you wouldn't forget me."

"It's been ten years. You look different." As a teenager, he was lanky, with dark-rimmed glasses and shaggy hair. The glasses he wears now are more sophisticated and fit his professional appearance.

"There's not a day that goes by that I don't think of you." West's deep voice halts my perusal of him and cause goosebumps to rise on my arms.

I'm speechless for a moment before saying, "That's quite an admission."

He lifts a broad shoulder and drops it. "I'm not ashamed to remain" — he pauses, appearing to mull over his words before finishing — "infatuated with you."

"After all these years?"

"It will forever be you."

His declaration sinks in and embeds itself into the marrow of my bones.

"I can't believe you'd do all this for Dana and me."

"I'd do anything to keep you with me."

My mouth drops open in shock. Not knowing how to respond, I let my eyes do the talking as they take in every inch of him. Everything from his perfectly styled hair, piercing blue eyes, to his designer suit with elegant cufflinks, down his long, muscular legs, and to his shiny black shoes.

"You look amazing," I say with the utmost honesty.

I always thought he was cute, but in a nerdy boy next door kind of way. I secretly harbored a crush on him throughout the high school years we spent together. Other than a lingering touch here or there, West made no moves to make me his girlfriend. The first time he kissed me was his last day on our island. Sure, we'd flirt, but it felt like a natural part of our friendship. I guess neither of us wanted to mess up what we had. Because what we had was amazing. Despite not dating, my relationship with West ran deep, as if he became a piece of my heart.

Now, he looks like he walked straight out of some hybrid issue of J. Crew and a bodybuilder magazine.

"You are even more beautiful than I remember. These past ten years have been good to you." His kind words send warmth to my cheeks.

I scan him again, trying and failing to calm my nerves and the thoughts infiltrating my overstimulated brain. In our five years together, Brad never made me feel like this. And he never kissed me with the passion West did on his last day in Emerald Springs.

"I can't believe you're here."

He chuckles. "Well, I do own it. So…" He turns his head away from me, but I don't miss the proud smile on his lips.

"It, as in…?" I ask.

"This resort and the island."

My eyebrows raise at that. "You've always been ambitious but owning your own island is…" I trail off, unsure of how to finish that thought.

His focus snaps back to me. "You think I'm ambitious?"

"Definitely. If you can pull off running the most exclusive resort in the world, you must have some ambition. You always put your all into everything you ever did. Academics, band, even your failed attempt at skateboarding." I can't help but smirk at the memory of West's tall form attempting to balance on a skateboard.

"You promised you'd never speak about 'the incident' again." He puts the incident in air quotes.

27

"I couldn't resist."

"In all seriousness, you were always the one pushing me to keep at it. Except when it came to skateboarding, but that was a hopeless case." His playful smile hasn't changed.

"So I can take some credit for this? How about a partial share?" I wink, teasing him. But something flashes in his eyes. I'm afraid I've upset him, so I add, "I'm only joking. You deserve all this and more."

His nostrils flare. I assume he's angry, but he says, "So do you."

"What?" I ask.

"You think I didn't notice your gift and passion?"

Suddenly, I feel too hot. He means my stories. I caught him once flipping through the pages of one of my notebooks. It was a romance about a girl named Olive and a boy named Easton. Not the most subtle way of writing down my own dreams of a happily ever after with Weston Lockwood. I grabbed the notebook from him and closed it, holding it tight to my chest. The smirk he wore did nothing to calm my racing heart. If he realized the similarities between the characters and us, he never told me.

"Your way with words was exceptional. I hope you kept pursuing your dream."

Embarrassment washes over me. "Privately, yes. Publicly, no."

"You never published?"

"I wrote more for my own creative outlet, not because I thought anyone else would be interested in reading." I don't mention that not a single manuscript has been completed. Not since high school. Not since he left.

"If a guy like me, who hated reading, was invested in your characters, I know people who love romance would absolutely adore everything you write."

"Thank you," I whisper.

An awkward silence passes.

"Shall we?" West asks, motioning to the door. "I think I owe your sister an apology as well. Although, I think she recognized me."

"I thought you looked like someone I knew but I don't think my heart was ready to admit it." I don't tell him the full truth.

"I hurt you back then."

It's not a question, so I say nothing.

"I'm sorry." He looks down at the floor, then back into my eyes. "I never meant to hurt you. But I had to leave."

"Why?"

His expression is pained when he answers. "I just had to."

"You're not going to tell me?" I ask.

"I want to. I plan to. But let me just enjoy seeing you after ten years of being apart first."

Anger replaces any empathy. I punch the button for the elevator and it opens.

As we step in, I whisper, "You're the one who left."

"I will explain myself. I will tell you everything, just give me time."

"I'm only here for a week." Although my heart is begging me to stay in the presence of the one who got away. *Ran away. West ran away from you.* Despite my heart's pleas to hear him out and get lost in his dreamy eyes, I turn and look out the glass elevator at the shore.

"Give me this week."

"For what?" I throw over my shoulder, refusing to face him.

"To convince you to stay."

My heart pounds hard and fast at the idea of moving miles and hours away from home. But something inside me yearns to give West this chance, this week, to win back what's always been his.

FOUR

West

Age 15

Olivia Swann is my teenage dream.

I've seen her around school with the football players and her fellow cheerleaders. But she never looks happy. Sure, she's smiling, but it looks forced.

Not that I know her well enough to assume her smile is forced, but something tells me she doesn't wear her genuine smile for those people. I glimpsed it in study hall while she wrote in her tattered notebook. I sat a few desks over from her and couldn't fight the urge to look at her as her hand flew across the page, scribbling down her thoughts like they'd float away if she didn't write them fast enough. She must have noticed my stare, because she looked up and our gazes collided. But she didn't scowl or look away. She stared right back and smiled, then turned her focus back to her notebook. All it took was those few seconds, and I was hooked.

Students swarm the courtyard during our lunch break. I've found my favorite spot on the edge of the field beneath a maple tree. Olivia steps out of the cafeteria and appears to scan her surroundings, as if she's looking for someone. Today is game day, which means she's wearing her cheer-leading uniform that shows off her toned legs.

Her eyes land on me, and she smiles, then waves. I turn to look behind me, checking to see if there's someone else she could be approaching. But I'm the only one here and before I know it, she stands over me, her backpack over her shoulder and lunch bag in her hand.

"Mind if I sit here?" she asks, and I nod my approval.

When she sits beside me, she tugs down her skirt despite the shorts peeking out from beneath.

"Thanks." She smiles and takes out her lunch — an egg salad sandwich, a bag of chips, and a bottle of water.

"I'm Olivia." When she extends her hand, I take it. Her skin is silky smooth. My heartbeat pulses in my ears.

I don't release her hand for several breaths, sucked into the pools of her amber eyes.

Olivia looks down at our hands, then back into my face; a pretty pink blush coats her cheeks. Reluctantly, I release her hand.

"You're West, right? West Lockwood? This is your first year at Emerald High?"

I nod and her brows scrunch together adorably at the center. She opens her mouth as if to say something but bites into her sandwich instead.

She chews for a few moments, swallows, then says, "I think we have some classes together. You're in homeroom with Mr. Henderson, too, right?"

I take a bite of my food as she asks the question. "Yeah." My voice comes out mumbled and I internally flinch. Embarrassment flares when I realize I'm talking to her with food in my mouth.

She takes a sip from her water bottle. Her lips quirk up in a half-smile. "You *can* speak then."

This is my chance to talk to the prettiest girl I've ever seen. If I keep up this silent act, she's going to leave. And I wouldn't blame her.

"I can," I reply. "I'm just not a big talker."

She smiles. "That's okay, I can probably talk enough for the both of us."

Olivia makes it sound like we're a team and my chest warms at that thought.

"Sounds good to me."

We eat in companionable silence. She makes no moves to leave, and I can sense she's comfortable around me. I don't understand why, but I'm not complaining.

Before I can work up the courage to say anything, she asks, "Are you going to the after-game party tonight?"

"No." My stomach rolls at the thought.

"Me neither."

"Why?" I ask.

Olivia glances away. "Parties aren't really my scene."

"Really?" I'm unable to hide my surprise.

She faces me. Her dark gold eyes pierce through my defenses. Olivia doesn't seem to be put off by my short answers. Unlike most kids our age, she doesn't fill up the silence with meaningless small talk. We're similar in that way. Already it feels like she can see through my awkwardly quiet exterior to who I am underneath. That's a crazy thought, but it's the only thing that explains why she's still sitting with me.

"They use any excuse they can to get rowdy. I don't drink or smoke or really care if our team wins or loses."

"You don't care if they win or lose, yet you're a cheer-leader?" I ask skeptically.

She smirks. "I like the stunts." Before I can comment further, she asks me another question. "Will you be at the game?"

"Yeah, I'm in the band."

She brightens, and it takes me off guard. Cheerleaders don't usually get excited about band members. "What do you play?"

"Drums."

"I see. All of this" — she motions toward me — "makes a lot more sense. Drummers are always the quiet, broody ones."

I can't help but smile. "I'm quiet, but I'm not broody."

She leans forward and her lavender perfume wafts around me, setting me more at ease. "You're acting pretty broody to me." She raises a perfectly sculpted eyebrow and sits back.

Olivia Swann is flirting with me, and it gives me a surge of confidence. "If you're not going to the after-game party, come to my house and watch a movie with me."

Her eyebrows shoot up and a wide smile stretches across her pouty lips. It looks way more authentic than the smiles she shares with her friends.

The bell rings and I stand, reaching down for her to take my hand. She places her small hand in mine and I pull her up with too much vigor. Stumbling forward, her free hand lands on my chest and she blinks up at me. That pretty pink blush covers her cheeks again, giving me another wave of confidence.

"Sorry," she mumbles, then takes a step back.

"What do you say? Are you gonna come to my house tonight?" I ask. My voice comes out deeper than normal. It's full of longing that I hope she doesn't catch.

We both bend down to pick up our trash. I take hers from her.

She nods. "I'll bring the pizza."

I try to argue, but she stops me by putting her hand up and insisting she'll provide the food. I toss our trash in the garbage can as she types my address into her notes and my number into her contacts. One of the jocks slides out from the side of the building and flicks his cigarette into the garbage.

"I hope you put that out first, Washburn," Olivia calls to him as he enters the building.

He waves a dismissive hand. Olivia mutters something under her breath.

My phone buzzes.

"That's me." Olivia nods toward my phone. "So you have my number too." She slips her hand in the crook of my elbow as we step through the doors and I puff out my chest, knowing that the prettiest girl in school is on my arm. The jocks stare at us in shock.

Too soon, we reach her locker. She gives my forearm a gentle squeeze and whispers just loud enough for me to hear, "I'll see you tonight."

FIVE

Olivia

Age 15

Someone took over my body at lunch. That's the only logical explanation I can come up with. Never in my life have I approached a boy. Sure, West is nerdy, but like a Clark Kent sort of nerdy. When I talk to guys at school, it's because they're my friends' boyfriends or because they approached me first.

But West is this quiet, broody boy that I am drawn to. I've caught him staring at me a few times. Most of the time when I meet his gaze, he looks away. Yesterday, he didn't. When I caught him staring in study hall, he locked me in and I couldn't look away. I didn't want to.

There's something about Weston Lockwood that has me wanting to know more. Not just because he's a geeky sort of adorable but because I sense there's something special about him. Something more. I want to figure out what that "more" is.

Those dark-rimmed glasses work for him. If the other girls looked past the lenses, they'd get lost in his ocean blue eyes. Just like I did. The girls in our school are too shallow to look past glasses, though. It's wrong of me to say, but it's true. I hope he never gets contacts because I want to keep Weston Lockwood all to myself.

My palms are sweating as I stand on his porch and ring his doorbell. It's not just from the hot pizza in my hands, either. West makes me nervous, a giddy kind of nervous, and my jittery nerves make my hands sweat.

Thankfully, I only live one street over and walked here. I'm not old enough to get my license and Mom and Dad went out on a date after the game and won't be home until well after one a.m. Dana is sleeping over at a friend's house, so I didn't have to answer any of my family's prying questions about West.

His house is an impressive red brick two-story colonial with white shutters. Their front yard is well maintained, with various shrubs and flowers throughout the flowerbeds. Mom showed a few people this house the first week it was on the market, but the Lockwood family snagged it before anyone else could make an acceptable offer.

West's front door swings open and a woman I assume is West's mom greets me. "You must be Olivia. I'm Sally Lockwood."

"It's nice to meet you, Mrs. Lockwood."

She waves me off. "No, none of that Mrs. Lockwood nonsense. Please call me Sally."

Sally ushers me in, and I follow her through the ornate entryway and down the first hall.

"West is in the kitchen."

Before we reach the kitchen, West emerges with a short stack of paper plates and napkins.

"Hey, Olivia," he says, glancing between me and his mom.

"Hi, West." I raise my hand in a wave and almost drop the pizza. Feeling like a klutz, I slide my hand beneath the pizza box to steady it.

West and I stand and stare at each other for a few beats, both of us apparently unsure of what to say or how to act. It's his mom who breaks the tension.

"You two kids have fun. West, don't forget to turn off the projector when you're done."

"Will do."

"It was nice meeting you, Olivia. Make yourself at home."

"Thank you."

After Sally disappears up the stairs, West motions for me to follow him. He opens the double doors at the end of the hall and I step into an actual theater room.

"Wow," I say, my eyes roaming over the five rows of leather couches. A screen descends from the ceiling.

"My dad is a huge movie buff."

"This is amazing. Those couches look crazy comfortable." I set the pizza down on the table next to where West set the plates and napkins.

A lopsided smile stretches across his lips, revealing his perfect teeth. "They are. What movie do you want to watch?"

"What do you have?" I ask, plating a slice of pizza on each of our two plates.

Nonchalantly, he says, "All of them." He motions to the plates. "You don't have to do that, I can get my own."

I wave him off. "It's no big deal. But you seriously have every movie?" I ask, making my way to the couch in the center row.

West shrugs. "My dad's a professional movie critic. So we have any movie that's come out in like the last fifteen years."

"That's too much pressure. Surprise me." I sit down but hold on to both plates.

West disappears behind a curtain for a few moments—where I assume the movies and projector are set up—and emerges when the movie's intro starts playing.

"Do you want soda or water?"

"Water, please," I answer.

After grabbing two bottles of water from the mini fridge, he strides over and takes the seat right next to me. I hand him his pizza and he thanks me before we turn our attention to the screen.

He chose an action movie with a romance subplot that keeps me invested.

After we both eat our fill of pizza, we settle back in our seats, our arms brushing. I rest my hand on the knee next to his, hoping he'll take the hint and lace his fingers in mine. He doesn't and I ignore the pang of disappointment.

He inches closer to me as the movie plays. His warmth permeates the sweatshirt and jeans I changed into after the game.

Several times, I fight the urge to rest my head on his shoulder. Instead, I focus on the movie and get pulled into the drama unfolding on screen.

After the heroine is kidnapped, the hero goes after the villain and several dramatic fight scenes unfold. The hero wins the final fight and saves the heroine from a cruel fate. The lovers are reunited and despite the hero being covered in blood and dirt, the heroine kisses him as if it's her last day on earth. The movie ends and the credits roll.

We turn to face each other. I tuck one leg beneath me. I expect him to say something, but he remains silent.

My silent West.

"How do you like Emerald High so far?" I ask.

"The end of my first week was way better than the start," he answers.

"Oh, yeah?"

"Everyone ignored me all week until this cheerleader showed up under my tree at lunch and invited herself to my house."

My mouth drops open. "I did not invite myself." I playfully poke him in the chest. "You invited me."

He grabs my finger and slides his palm over mine, staring at our hands pressed together. His skin against mine sets my heart racing and head spinning.

"Who said I was talking about you?" His voice is husky.

I pull my hand away, immediately missing our connection, and scoot back. Crossing my arms over my chest, I ask, "Oh, another one of the cheerleaders invited themselves here tonight?" Despite knowing he's just teasing me, jealousy churns in my gut.

It vanishes the moment West reaches forward and brushes a strand of hair behind my ear.

"No. No one else even *saw* me this week. At least not until you were on my arm." His fingers linger on my chin and my insides turn to liquid at the gentleness of his touch.

As his hand slips away, his eyes drift down to my lips.

"I guess we'll see how next week goes. Maybe one of the other cheerleaders will steal you from me."

"That's never going to happen." His eyes scan my face and warmth fills me.

"No?" I ask. My voice is breathless, and I'd be embarrassed if I was with anyone else. West should feel like a stranger. But he doesn't. Not at all. He feels like my person.

"You're stuck with me now." His lips tilt into a half smile.

"Sounds good to me."

We sit and talk for a long time. Well, I talk, but West opens up a little more. He's not as tight-lipped as he was at lunch. This boy is a puzzle I enjoy piecing together. After his grandfather clock chimes twelve, I decide I need to get home before my parents get back from their date night and discover I'm not there.

I don't have a curfew, but tonight is pushing it.

Spending this time with Weston Lockwood was worth it, though.

I slap my hands on my thighs and stand. "Well, I should get home."

He stands and says, "My mom can drive you."

"No, that's okay. I walked here."

"I'll walk you home."

"It's not far. I don't want to put you out."

He gives me a look. "Walking you home doesn't put me out. It's a good excuse to spend more time with you."

My heart pitter patters at that. I bite my lip. "You don't need to find an excuse to spend time with me. I enjoy your company."

He slides his glasses back up his nose. "Really?"

"Does that surprise you?" I ask.

"Yeah, actually."

"Why?"

"Girls like you don't typically give guys like me a second glance." The honesty in his tone humbles me.

"Girls like me?"

"Pretty, popular, a cheerleader."

"You think I'm pretty?" I ask, batting my eyelashes, trying to make light of the butterflies taking over my insides.

"Pretty isn't a strong enough word."

I shake my head and mumble a thank you.

In another surprising act of boldness, West touches my chin and angles my head up so we're once again eye to eye.

"Let me walk you home." The gentle command has me nodding my approval.

Our arms swing between us as we make our way to my house. When we reach my front door, I dig my keys out of my purse, but before I have the chance to unlock the door, West stops me. I turn to face him, heart thundering in my chest, waiting for him to make the first move.

My hands are clasped in his as he runs his thumbs over the backs.

"Thank you for hanging out with me tonight."

"I hope it's not the last time we hang out," I say, hoping he hears the sincerity in my words.

His eyebrows raise and his glasses slide down his nose with the action. After releasing one of my hands, he pushes them back into place.

"It won't be," he says confidently. He leans forward and tucks back a strand of hair that escaped from my messy bun. It's the second time he's touched my hair tonight, and I'm not complaining.

"Good," I whisper.

He brushes a hand down the side of my face and my breath halts. My eyes fall closed.

"Good night, Olivia," he whispers, and my eyes flutter open when he releases his hold on me.

Another pang of disappointment hits me, but I ignore it. Instead, I focus on being grateful for my budding friendship with the new mysterious drummer boy.

SIX

West

Present

The slightest brush of Olivia's arm against mine is like a direct hit to my nervous system. She smells like the vanilla lavender candles my mom used to burn. Despite her obvious anger toward me, I feel grateful for this potential opportunity. Even if I crash and burn, God has answered part of my prayer.

When the concierge, Mindy, knocked on my office door and informed me there were two guests who lost their room due to a double booking, I thought my newest employee was being naive. People are always trying to get in without making a reservation. But when she explained they were the guests who booked the private plane package and then asked for me by name, I didn't have a choice but to handle the issue myself.

I walked to the front desk and Mindy pointed to the names of the supposed double-booked reservation. My eyes landed on Olivia Swann and Brad Washburn with the asterisk beside their names, noting they had a honeymoon suite, and it felt like someone had taken a sledgehammer to my chest.

Olivia's social media pages revealed they were engaged and that their wedding was scheduled for yesterday. But this is the last place I thought they'd go on their honeymoon. I don't advertise this resort. My marketing is via word of mouth. We have a website for online reservations, but that's it. One reason it's so exclusive is because our guests want full privacy. It's the way it was when I took it over and the reason I invested in this resort — I want my own privacy.

So, no, I did not expect to see a couple from my old town here at my resort. Let alone the woman I loved on her honeymoon with my high school nemesis.

But when it was Dana I saw on Olivia's arm as they approached me at the front desk, all I felt was relief. Until Dana informed me of Olivia's predicament and how she had experienced the ultimate betrayal less than forty-eight hours ago.

I steal a glance at Olivia's reflection. Her eyes sparkle as they sweep over the landscape. As if she's fallen in love with this place as quickly as I did.

The elevator dings and I focus on the opening doors before she catches me staring. Having her here with me is better than I could have hoped for. Our history is something I'll never forget but our future is what matters most. Before I plan our future, I need to focus on the present. Right now, she's furious and confused, and I need to make things right.

It's been ten years, but she's here with me. At my resort, on my island, and I will do everything in my power to keep her here.

We step out into the foyer and Dana storms over to us, wielding a bread knife.

"Oh, it's just you." She wipes her brow. "I thought you were one of those rogue resort employees."

"You need to stop listening to those true crime podcasts," Olivia deadpans.

Dana looks between Olivia and me. "Wait. It's you and West."

Olivia's eyes widen. "So you did recognize him!"

"Maybe." Dana gives me a side eye.

None of us speaks for several long breaths.

I cross my arms and finally break the silence. "Did you have something to do with this?"

Olivia copies my pose.

Dana puts her hands up in defense. "I did not plan this honeymoon, if that's what you're asking."

"You refused to cancel the reservation." Olivia turns on Dana. "Why?"

Dana shrugs. "I told you. Everything was non-refundable."

"It says on the website there are certain exceptions. Like a canceled wedding," I say.

Dana's eyes go round, as if she knows she's been caught. "Okay, fine. When I looked up the phone number for the resort, I saw that Weston Lockwood owned it. So instead of canceling everything, I convinced you to take me, instead. I wasn't going to pass up the opportunity to reconnect you two."

Despite the lies she told to get Olivia here, I can't help but feel grateful for Dana's meddling.

"To be fair, I didn't realize you were going to give up your home to keep us at your resort," Dana says.

I lift a shoulder and drop it. "When I realized who you were, I knew I had to make sure you were both taken care of."

"You've always been thoughtful. I shouldn't be surprised that you'd give up your space for us, but that's still very generous of you." The sincerity in Dana's voice makes heat creep up my neck. I loosen my tie.

Dana turns to her sister, her smile growing larger by the second.

"There it is," she says, gently shoving Olivia's shoulder.

"There what is?" Olivia asks.

"The inner radiance that only West has ever brought out of you."

Olivia's cheeks turn a pretty shade of pink.

I remember seeing her around school that first week and how she never appeared comfortable with her so-called friends. Even then, it's like I knew her. She had a distinct glow about her once we started spending more time together. I never took credit for it, but maybe Dana is on to something.

Dana drops her arms to her sides. "It's why you practically glimmered walking around every summer you spent together. You two were inseparable."

She's not wrong. Every waking moment, I wanted to be with Olivia. So every moment I could be with her, I was. Every football game, I was there in the stands, watching her as she cheered, proud to be best friends with the kindest and prettiest girl at school. The summers were even better. We'd spend sunrise to sunset together, and often even later than that.

For the last ten years, she's been the center of my prayers.

"Brad only ever dimmed your light," Dana continues, seemingly oblivious to the hurt etching its way onto Olivia's face at the mention of her ex.

Needing something to change the subject, I ask, "Why don't you two sit down and I'll make us some coffee?"

The girls nod their approval.

"Do you still make it with a dash of cinnamon and nutmeg?" I direct my question to Olivia.

"How did you remember such a mundane thing?" Olivia asks.

I shrug off my suit jacket and drape it over one of the chairs at the kitchen island. After unbuttoning my cuffs, I roll up my sleeves.

"When it comes to you, there's not a thing I've forgotten."

Leaving Olivia was the hardest thing I've ever done. From here on out, I vow to do everything I can to make up for the last ten years. Starting with making her coffee exactly how she likes it.

"I take mine the same, not that you asked." Dana shoots me a glare.

"I was going to ask you next," I tell her.

"Sure you were." Dana rolls her eyes, and it takes me back to the attitude teenage Dana gave her parents when they asked her to do the simplest of chores.

"You haven't changed," I say.

"Well, you have, and I haven't decided if that's a good thing or not," Dana retorts.

I chuckle and make quick work of getting fresh grounds into the filter with a pinch of cinnamon and nutmeg, stirring the grounds and spices together, then pour the water into the coffee maker.

As it percolates, Dana catches me up on all the goings on in my old town. Not that there is much. She never brings up the fire, and I'm grateful.

Olivia reaches for my Bible and slides it over from where I set it down and runs her finger over the spine and traces the lettering spelling out Holy Bible.

"So, when did you become a Christian?" Olivia asks, cutting her sister off from sharing more gossip.

"I came to know Jesus after I survived a shark attack." I pour a healthy dose of creamer into Olivia's mug and hand it to her. After I drop a sugar cube into another mug and get the cream out of the refrigerator, I pour a little into Dana's coffee. "Is this still how you take it?" I push the mug across the marble countertop to Dana.

Both women stare at me open mouthed.

"Shark attack?" Dana asks. "Explain. Full story. Now."

This girl truly hasn't changed. She's the same spitfire I remember.

"I went out surfing and the tide pulled me deeper than I've ever been before. After catching a powerful wave, I lost my balance and fell in. I cut my ankle on the board. Apparently, there was a shark nearby. He grabbed my ankle, and I screamed, begging God to save me. Without thinking, I used my other foot to kick it in the eye and he released me. The kick stunned it enough to back off. I have a scar from where the shark bit me to show for it, but other than some stitches, I came out unscathed."

"You just *kicked* it in the eyeball? Like without passing out?" Olivia asks, then adds, "I would have totally passed out and become the shark's unhappy meal."

Picturing Olivia in the jaws of a great white is the last thing I want on my mind, so I pour myself a cup of coffee while I finish the story. "It was like I temporarily lost control of my body. I kicked it hard enough to stupefy it and before I knew what was happening, the perfect wave came and I rode it to shore on my knees. After a quick trip to the hospital and dodging news crews, I found a church, tracked down the pastor, and asked him how to become a Christian. Any doubts about God caring about me vanished when He answered my desperate prayer."

Olivia has a shocked smile. Dana's mouth is still hanging open. I lift my black coffee to my lips and take a sip.

"That's quite a story," Olivia says.

"It is."

"Which is all it is, a story. Right? There's no way you got out of a shark attack in the middle of the ocean and had the perfect wave save you." Her skepticism is evident in her voice.

"God works miracles. He has a way of doing things we'd never imagine possible." I take another sip of coffee.

"I'm aware," Olivia says.

"Just like this" — I point between us — "wasn't fate. I've been praying for you for the last ten years and asking God to bring you to me. For Him to give me another chance with the girl who I had to leave behind."

Hurt flashes in her eyes. "Prove it."

"Prove what?"

"Everything."

I am ready and excited to see the look on her face when I reveal the proof. I open the drawer stuffed full of takeout menus and random newspaper clippings.

"Despite my efforts to keep the attack out of the news, someone from the hospital snagged the pictures of my injuries from my hospital account and sent them to the paper."

I hand it over to her. She scans it for a moment before handing it back to me.

"Okay, that's proof enough for that. Now I'd like to see you prove the other part."

"You don't believe that I've prayed for you every day for ten years?"

"It's not like you can prove that, anyway."

I motion for my Bible and she slides it over to me. I open its pages and pull out the notes on scrap pieces of paper that I've written over the years. There are dozens, but I think six should do the trick. I pluck a few out and hand them over to her.

She begins to read the first one out loud. "December 16, 2017. Lord, I pray Olivia comes to know you." After the first line, she stares at the paper. She looks up at me and there are tears in her eyes. "You prayed for me… and God answered your prayer."

"What?"

"I had my Jesus moment on December 17, 2017. It's a day I'll never forget. Everything was overwhelming and I felt like

I'd never make it through. I knew I couldn't do it anymore on my own. That day I threw up my hands in defeat and asked Jesus to take control. From then on, my life changed forever. After that, I knew that no matter what life threw at me, with Jesus on my side, I'd get through it and move on." She says no more about it and as much as I'd love to hear her testimony, she doesn't look ready to share.

Warmth spreads through me. I want to wrap her in my arms and hold her, thanking God for saving her. It's hard to believe God answered my prayer the day after I wrote it, but then again, God never works in the ways or time we expect Him to.

"So do you believe me?" I ask.

Olivia purses her lips to the side but says nothing.

There's one prayer, a desperate, vulnerable prayer, that she needs to hear.

Opening my Bible to the last page, I pull out the note I wrote two nights ago. "God, I'm struggling. She's marrying the guy who bullied me through high school tomorrow. I've forgiven him, but it hurts to know my chance with her is gone. Help me accept their marriage and move on." The pen color changes from black to blue, showing where I came back to finish the prayer several hours later that night. "But God, if it be your will, give me one last chance with her. I know it's a selfish prayer, but I'm restless. I can't sleep. Something tells me there's something going on. If this is just a sinful, selfish hope, forgive me and help me move past this. But God, if it's real… protect her. Pull her into Your arms and give her peace. And if it's real… Please give me another chance. Your Word says You give us the desires of our heart if our heart is aligned with You. And Olivia Swann has been the desire of my heart since I was fifteen years old." I fold the paper and slide it back into place, then swallow the lump in my throat.

Laying myself bare and wide open to a possible hideous rejection has destroyed any confidence I had.

Any hope I've clung to disappears as Olivia turns and walks away from me. Leaving the heart I just poured out to her twitching on the floor.

SEVEN

West

And just like that, my second chance with Olivia Swann has crashed and burned.

I wave goodbye to her sister, the spectator to my heart's destruction, and leave without another word. I already humiliated myself enough for a lifetime.

Finding out Olivia never wanted me in the same way I wanted her shouldn't have surprised me as much as it did. Even with all the money I have, I'm not enough for her. I never have been and never will be.

"I'll never be worthy," I mutter to myself.

"You don't need to be," a still quiet voice reminds me.

My phone beeps with a new email. I open it and read the message.

Someone wants to book a last-minute wedding ceremony on the beach. They are offering an obscene amount of money, too.

I reply to the email chain and tell my assistant to have the only available accommodation cleaned and prepped for our new guests. I could have prepared the vacant bungalow for Olivia and Dana, but once I learned it was the Swann sisters who were double-booked, I knew my penthouse was the better option for their stay.

Not that it matters now.

I bottle my embarrassment and rejection, putting it away to be absorbed later. Now isn't the time to dwell on what almost was. Now I need to focus on work.

When I reach the check-in desk, Mindy is with a guest. I step through the door and walk to my office.

"Mr. Lockwood, wait," Mindy calls to me. "Our guest, Mr. Washburn, asked to speak to a manager." My blood freezes in my veins.

"Lockwood? As in West Lockwood?" Brad's familiar voice booms from the lobby.

Mindy nods to our newest guest and I clench my eyes closed.

"No way! It's been years, man."

My gut rolls and I'm transported back to high school, where Brad and his minions battered what little confidence I had.

Where my self-worth was at an all-time low and the only light in my darkness was a girl named Olivia Swann. Just like that, I'm brought back to reality, where Olivia Swann rejected me when I was at my most vulnerable and I am face to face with her ex-fiancé.

Brad looks me over with a demeaning smile. "This is a nice place."

"Thanks," I grit through my teeth.

"You've created quite an empire here, haven't you?"

I say nothing.

"Have you found anyone to share this with? You know Olivia and I settled down together, right? Have you seen her recently?"

Brad fires the questions in rapid succession.

"I think you mean you failed to settle down with Olivia when you cheated on her." His smile turns into a scowl, and I fire my own question without answering one of his. "Why are you here?"

"Brad?" Olivia's shocked voice cuts in before Brad can answer.

He turns to face her. She has my jacket draped over her arm, and her eyes are puffy and rimmed in red.

"What are you doing here?" she asks him.

"To do what I've planned to do for the last two years."

She crosses her arms, clutching my jacket to her chest.

"What's that? Sleep with more of my bridesmaids?"

Brad looks irritated, not ashamed. "Liv Bug, don't do this. You had it all planned out. A ceremony at sunset on the beach. Our family and friends together, creating an intimate audience as you became my wife."

Olivia shakes her head. "No, Brad. You destroyed that when you slept with Lexi."

Several heads turn in their direction. I step back into the lobby, giving the nosier patrons a fake smile and a nod to keep them away.

"Why don't you take this somewhere more private?" I suggest, ushering them out of the lobby.

They both agree and I show them to the smallest conference room, since it's the only one available.

Brad doesn't wait for me to leave. "I have needs that you've failed to meet. Lexi was there and willing."

Despite the damage Olivia did to my heart less than an hour ago, I can't help but feel protective of her. "You're blaming Olivia for your infidelity?"

"Shut it, super dork."

"No, you shut it, Brad!" Brad's mouth snaps closed at Olivia's tone. "You knew when we started dating that I wanted to wait. You told me it was important to you too."

"I screwed up, okay? I know and I'm sorry. My need outweighed my rational thoughts."

I scoff at his pathetic apology. If Brad hears me, he doesn't show it.

Olivia's jaw clenches and her nostrils flare. Despite the seriousness of this moment, I can't help but find her adorable.

He stalks toward her. My shoulders stiffen and all my muscles tense. She takes several steps backward until her back is pressed against my front. Instinctively, I wrap my arm around her waist, giving her my silent support.

She tilts her head back to look up at me and the trust that shines in her eyes kicks my protective instinct into overdrive and makes me forget about the heart she broke only minutes ago.

Brad starts on a tangent about how her parents are losing tons of money on a ceremony and reception that will never happen because of her lack of forgiveness. I can see her crumbling under the weight of his accusations.

"Get out," I growl, pointing at the door.

"You won't tell me what to do."

"Get. Out." My words are clipped and full of warning.

"Not without my Olive." He grabs her wrist and tugs at her so forcefully she's ripped out of my grip. She cries out in pain and all I see is red.

In the blink of an eye, I have my hand curled around his wrist, pressing my thumb into a pressure point that numbs his entire arm. He releases her and she stumbles back but rights herself quickly. I press harder and the pain sends him to his knees. I stare down at him, grateful for my single semester of Krav Maga.

"Tell her you're sorry," I demand.

"Get your hands off me! I'm calling the police!"

I keep my thumb firmly on his pressure point. "The only two witnesses are me and the woman you just manhandled. What exactly are you going to tell the police?"

"That you attacked me!" Brad shouts.

Olivia laughs. "Seriously?"

"Yeah, seriously. My arm is numb."

"And you squeezed my wrist so hard I'm going to bruise. Do you really want to go into that battle?" Olivia lifts her arm to show Brad the marks. When my eyes land on the outline of Brad's fingers on her skin, red floods my vision. My spirit immediately settles after a three-word, silent prayer: "God help me."

"Leave Olivia alone."

Brad lashes out. "You're pathetic. You both are. Always have been."

"Okay," Olivia says, looking bored.

As much as I want to twist his wrist until tears stream down his cheeks, I don't. Instead, I release him.

I step beside Olivia, needing her close, to know she's okay.

Brad rubs his arm that must be numb and looks at Olivia. "I'm sorry. I'm sorry I wasted five years of my life on you. I'm sorry I ever thought you were worth anything."

That final blow strikes a nerve. Pain replaces the calm on Olivia's face. Her eyes well with tears.

I take a threatening step forward. "Say you're sorry and *mean it*." My voice leaves no room for argument.

"I'm sorry." He looks at me. "Good enough?"

"Not even close," I growl. Silently, I beg God for strength when all I want to do is rip Brad apart.

Olivia's hand on my arm gives me the calm I need.

"He's not worth it," she whispers.

As much as I agree with her, I can't let him off the hook without putting him in his place. "It's sad that you think you ever deserved Olivia. You've never been good enough for her and you know it," I say.

Brad stares at me with his signature sneer on his face. "Whatever. I'm done with you. Both of you." He nods to Olivia and leaves.

Once Brad is gone, I expect Olivia to leave or to ask me to leave. Instead, she throws herself into my arms and I wrap them around her. She buries her face in my chest and I sit down in one of the chairs with her curled on my lap.

"He was way out of line. I'm sorry he said those ugly things to you."

"I'm so sorry," she whispers with a sniffle.

"What could you possibly be sorry for?"

"I ran away when I should have stayed."

"With Brad?" I ask, too afraid to hope.

She pulls back to look up at me and scrunches her nose adorably. "No. I should have sprinted away from him years ago." She runs her finger over the pattern on my tie. "Earlier, I shouldn't have run. But you... you made me feel things, and it scared me."

"The last thing I want to do is scare you." I tip her chin up. "But when I'm in, I'm all in. And from the moment I laid eyes on you, I've been all in."

"It's been ten years." Her eyes look between mine.

I tuck a loose strand of hair behind her ear. "And in those ten years, God has blessed me beyond my wildest dreams. He's given me way more than I deserve. But there's been one thing I've prayed for desperately that He's kept out of my reach."

"Ruling the world?" she asks with a little smirk.

I stare deep into her eyes. "You."

Her mouth drops open with a surprised exhale. Her lips are like a magnet, pulling me in without permission. There's not an ounce of protest in me as she leans her face closer to mine. Her brown eyes blink up at me then drop to my lips. I watch in utter fascination as she licks her lower lip, her eyes still fixed on my mouth.

My breaths are ragged and my insides tighten. I am a single breath away from kissing Olivia Swann.

EIGHT

Olivia

"I knew it!" Brad bursts through the door, breaking the trance West put me under with his sweet words and shattering our almost-kiss.

I jump off West's lap, my entire body heating. "Knew what?" I ask.

"That he still has feelings for you. That's why I chose this resort — to put an end to his ridiculous crush."

"You knew? That's why you were so bent on coming here?" I ask, feeling my gut churn at Brad's endless layers of betrayal.

Brad doesn't look at me; he turns to West. "Yep. I wanted to make sure he knew his chance with you was over."

Tears blur my vision. I really thought Brad turned over a new leaf when we went to college. I hadn't heard a word from West for five years by then and figured it was time to give up on him and move on. I was so stupid to think Brad had become a different person overnight.

"And here you are, finding out it's you who no longer has a chance," I say with a haughty smile.

Brad's face falls for a second before his sneer returns. "What about you?"

"What about me?"

"Sure, I cheated on you, but you've clearly never stopped having feelings for West. Your cheating is even worse." He rests his hands on his hips.

I stiffen my spine. "That's a completely different scenario and you know it. I never acted on my feelings."

Brad changes topics. "Did West tell you why he moved? Or why his family vanished in the middle of the night?" Brad's taunting smile both sets me on edge and fuels my protective instinct. "He's not who you think he is," Brad warns.

"West is even more than I thought he was." I let my eyes roam over West. "I somehow forgot he has a heart of gold."

There's dual emotions in West's eyes: fear and desire. I'm not sure which one I see more of.

"Really?" I can see Brad shake his head from the corner of my eye. "You're drooling over a killer. Did you know that?"

Those words break me free of my ogling to look at Brad.

"Don't," West snaps at Brad.

"Don't? Are you kidding me? Did you really think I'd sit idly by while you stole my fiancée and not tell her the truth about you? It's another reason I chose this resort — to show Olivia once and for all who you really are."

"West?" I ask.

He closes his eyes, and his face is full of regret.

"West caused the fire that burned down the school administration building and killed Mr. Fields." Brad doesn't waste another second.

Suddenly, all the contents of my stomach turn sour. My mind runs through all the details my dad shared with me, and I conclude that Brad could be telling the truth. Maybe I don't know West as well as I thought I did.

"Is that true?" I direct my question to West.

He says nothing.

"That's why you moved away, isn't it?" I push.

"Yes." West's voice is full of pain. "No one blamed me. Not out loud, anyway."

"I blamed you. Most of the firemen blamed you. Even a handful of teachers knew it was your fault Mr. Fields died," Brad says.

"Shut up, Brad," I command.

"Excuse me?" Brad asks in a tone that tells me I'm walking a fine line.

"What happened at the admin building was an awful accident, but that's what it was ruled — an accident," I say.

"It was an accident, but it was my fault," West says. "I thought I blew the candle out before leaving Mr. Henderson's office, but I must have forgotten. It caught the curtains on fire and burned down half the building."

"The fire was caused by a cigarette in the trash can," I tell him.

"What?" West asks.

"Yeah, after a deeper investigation, they realized the candle wasn't the cause of the fire. It was a cigarette in a trash can," I explain.

"So I wasn't the one who caused—"

I shake my head. "Not unless you were the one who threw the cigarette into the trash." West shakes his head no, so I continue. "From what the report said, the candle wasn't lit. Mr. Henderson confirmed he came back into the office after you had left and the candle was out. None of that was your fault."

West's expression is unreadable.

"That's a lie!" Brad shouts. Despite his harsh tone, fear fills his expression.

"Are you calling my dad a liar?" I ask Brad, anger building in my chest. My dad would never put his job as fire chief at risk.

"You're lying to make this loser feel better," Brad says.

I ignore Brad and his weak attempt at getting under West's skin.

"I'm not lying. I can call my dad right now and have him confirm the story."

"I trust you." West reaches for my hand and envelops my fingers in his warmth. He gives my hand a quick squeeze and steps away, pulling his phone from his pocket and calling someone.

"This is unreal." Brad throws his hands up in the air. "I came here to marry you, and instead you're taking this loser's side."

"You keep calling him a loser, but he's never been one. Just because he wasn't part of your group of jocks doesn't make him a loser. Not then, and certainly not now." I cross my arms and arch an eyebrow.

"Thanks," West says to the person on the other end of the line before he hangs up and tucks his phone back into his pocket. "Brad, I am going to tell you one more time — get out. You are not welcome at my resort or on this island. You can leave right now, or I can escort you off my island."

"*Your* island? You're joking, right? You made that up to look more important than you are." Brad's voice wavers, as if he isn't convinced by his own explanation.

"Brad, give up. You've lost. Accept that and move on. You lost me when you slept with Lexi. There's no coming back from that." He doesn't respond, so I ask him, "Why are you so obsessed with tearing West down? What did he ever do to you?"

Brad shoots a look at West, who looks as though he's trying to fit together a mental puzzle.

"He's dangerous, Liv."

"How?" I ask, irritated.

"Do you know why he moved to Emerald Springs in the middle of the school year?" Brad asks.

I peek over at West, who stands at attention once again.

"They arrested him for assault." Brad crosses his arms, as if he's challenging West to fight back.

To my horror, West doesn't say a word.

"Okay, Brad. Enough with the lies," I say, fighting down the anxiety that there may be at least some truth to Brad's accusations.

"Am I lying?" Brad directs his question to West.

"No." West's one word response has my mind reeling and my stomach rolling over.

I blink at West, questioning once again if my instincts about my best friend have been wrong for all these years.

"There's an explanation, right?"

"Yes." There's no hesitation in West's response. "Do you trust me?"

"Yes." That single word spouts from my lips without my consent. In my bones, I know it was the right answer.

Brad sneers and I suddenly realize how ugly my ex is on the inside. "You're many things, Olivia Swann, but I never took you for an idiot."

West stalks over to Brad, who stares up at him, his nose raised.

Back in high school, Brad was always the guy with the biggest muscles, domineering other guys with his brawn. But now, West's presence is more intimidating and powerful than Brad's ever was.

West grabs Brad by the collar and tugs him forward, mumbling something that I can't make out before he shoves him in the chest and says, "Out."

Brad backs away slowly, hands in the air as if he's surrendering. Once he's in the hallway, he puts his hands down. West walks to the door and I follow him, feeling a satisfied smile stretch across my lips as security surrounds Brad and escorts him out of the building.

"Assault, explain," I demand before West even turns back to face me.

His shoulders slump and he cups the back of his neck with both hands and turns. We go back into the conference room and I shut the door. West paces back and forth, his hands still gripping his neck.

He stops and faces me, but he looks past me. "It was two months into my freshman year and I was invited to my very first party. I spent most of the night on my own, only talking to people when they came over to me." Despite the seriousness of the moment, he gives me a wolfish grin. "You might remember this about me, but I wasn't much of a talker back then."

I bite my lip, attempting not to smile.

"Well, at one point, I wandered into the kitchen for another soda. Clint Denver, the town golden boy, didn't notice me in there. He poured a small packet of powder into a drink. I didn't want to get involved, but when I saw him hand it to a girl and wrap his arm around her waist, I couldn't sit idly by. So, I confronted him. He punched me in the jaw. I stumbled back and when he lunged for me again, I landed the next punch and broke his nose. There weren't many witnesses, but they were all his friends and they told the police I attacked him first. So, they charged me with assault. Being a minor, and it being my first offense, I only had to do community service." He rubs the scruff on his jaw.

"Is that why you moved to Emerald Springs?"

"Yes and no. Mom had her eye on Emerald Springs for a while, and since she and Dad worked remotely, we could up and move at the drop of a hat. Once I served my community service hours, we moved to Emerald Springs."

"Twice you've been uprooted because of things you're not guilty of."

West shrugs, the defeat on his face quickly replaced with something else. "Who knows? If I didn't go through that in Chicago, we never would have moved to Emerald Springs, and I never would have met you."

West places his hands on my shoulders. I look up at him and a powerful emotion overwhelms me. My memories of him didn't do him justice. I forgot how fiercely protective he is. Warmth and light and everything good fills my heart until it overflows.

"Everything happens for a reason," he says.

"You, of all people, would know that," I say. "For the last ten years, you've believed you killed Mr. Fields. Why didn't you fight to stay? Why didn't you wait for the final report?"

"I had convinced myself it was my fault. When I told my parents, they immediately called every attorney on the island. Every one of them refused to represent me after learning about my record. Someone from the station showed up with a letter signed by your dad and sealed by the mayor stating that if I left Emerald Springs and never showed my face again, they wouldn't press charges."

My brow furrows. "What? My dad would never do something like that."

West swallows. "It was his signature."

"And you changed your numbers so no one could have reached you to tell you it wasn't your fault. That there wouldn't be any charges." Anger brews at this new knowledge. I can't believe my dad would do something like that. I make a mental note to confront him the next time we talk.

"Are you upset?" I ask. West doesn't answer. He only looks at me thoughtfully and it reminds me of our first weeks as friends. He was so quiet. When he stays silent, I clarify, "That you've been living with guilt for something you didn't even do?"

"I want to say no. I know God had a plan for all of this. He always does. But I am a little irritated that it took ten years for my conscience to be clear of a murder."

"I didn't even know you were at the admin building that weekend."

West looks down, looking ashamed.

"I didn't think you were struggling with school. So why were you there?" I ask.

"Mr. Henderson was helping me work through some things."

He stops talking, so I don't push him. After a few minutes of silence, he goes on.

"I had — still have — pretty bad anxiety."

"Really?" I know anxiety manifests itself differently depending on the person, but West never showed any signs that I was aware of.

"Mr. Henderson really helped me. He used to burn a vanilla lavender candle during our sessions." West smirks and I realize why. "Being with you calmed me and you always smelled like vanilla lavender."

I inhale a shaky breath. "I'm so sorry you went through that. If I knew you ran because you thought the fire was your fault, I would have done everything I could to track you down. So you would have known the truth." The unfairness of it all weighs on me. I don't realize I'm crying until West wipes my tears away before he pulls me into his arms.

"Don't cry, sweetheart. Not for me."

"Too late." I chuckle. Countless nights I cried into my pillow over this man. For years, I believed he abandoned me. But I'm not crying because of my own pain this time. Now I'm crying for the pain he's been carrying for a decade.

"Please don't cry for me. I'm okay. And I'm not upset with your dad."

"You have every right to be."

"God's ways aren't always easy. Often, they're not. But He has a purpose for every ounce of pain." He licks his lips. "The pain I faced pales in comparison to the joy I feel now." West tightens his hold me. "The happiness I feel right now, with you in my arms, makes the pain of the last ten years worth it."

I rest my cheek on his chest, feeling utterly unworthy of this man. Despite this feeling, I try to lighten the mood. "I'm sure it didn't hurt that you also became a billionaire during that time."

His chuckle is deep and satisfying.

"Speaking of, I think it's time I do what I've wanted to do since becoming a billionaire."

I pull back, but keep my arms locked around him. "You've already bought an island. What's next, a country?"

He shakes his head with a smirk. "I want to spoil you. Let me take you on a proper date… in my helicopter."

"I don't need to be spoiled. You don't need to do anything crazy or extravagant for me," I say, despite the giddiness that fills me.

"What's the point of having all this money if I don't have anyone to share it with?"

"Why me?"

He pauses as though he wants to formulate his response in a way I'll understand. "You saw me when no one else did. Even though you were popular, you spent lunch with me. As a cheerleader, they expected you to go to the parties after games with the jocks and other cheerleaders, but you came to my house and ate terrible pizza instead. Your status in high school dropped because of me. But you prioritized me over that."

I lift a shoulder, then drop it. "Status in high school wasn't important to me. Besides, I could be myself with you. Being with you was always way more fun. Plus, your phenomenal movie selection made the pizza slightly less terrible."

West gives me a shy smile, reaching out his hand for me to take. "So, what do you say, Olivia Swann? Can I take you on a date?"

The moment my hand lands in his, warmth consumes me.

"Absolutely."

NINE

West

We've remained in the conference room, catching up on life. There are a million things I should be working on, but I'm not ready to leave her after finally getting her back.

"I'm not a killer," I say it out loud, still not believing the truth of that statement.

Olivia nods, but says nothing.

Staring past her, I add, "I never thought I would be able to say that with conviction." I turn to her, looking directly into her eyes. "Once again, thanks to you, I have found stability on unsteady ground."

Her brow furrows and she asks, "What?"

Before I knew Jesus, she was what I clung to when life set me on edge. She stood by me and, without realizing it, balanced me while I walked on a tightrope.

"When I had to leave you behind, it was worse than having a rug pulled out from beneath me. You were my lifeline in so many ways. Our late-night talks and walks on the beach made up for always feeling like the outcast. Knowing I had you in my corner despite my ranking in our status obsessed high school was what got me through. Then the fire happened… and I had to cut all ties to my lifeline — to you — and it felt like I was going to drown."

"It felt that way for me too," Olivia admits. Her eyes are watery; a tear rolls down her cheek.

Reaching forward, I swipe the tear off her cheek. "I'm sorry I left you."

"Me, too." She shakes her head, as if she's trying to rid her mind of the memories. "But these ten years have been good to you."

To the outside world, these last ten years have been the most successful years of my life. But there is more to life than money and material possessions.

"How in the world did this all come to be?" She waves her arms around, motioning to our surroundings.

"Do you remember my uncle Hans?" I ask.

She smirks and nods. "Yeah, that grumpy old man is impossible to forget."

Olivia had taken a trip or two with me back in high school to visit him. Uncle Hans took an immediate liking to her.

"Well, after he died, I found out my regular visits meant more to him than I realized. He left his fortune to me. When I turned eighteen, I became a millionaire. After some investing in the market and real estate, my uncle's millions turned into my billions, and I bought this resort and then the island."

Olivia's eyebrows raise at that. "Wow." She stares at me for several seconds, her expression shifting from wonder to sadness. "Why didn't you come back after all that?"

"I planned to, actually. When I finally worked up the courage to disregard your dad's letter, I found you on social media and saw that you were engaged to Brad. You were the most important reason, the only reason, really, that I wanted to come back. But you were engaged to another man. So I stayed away." I wanted to go back and claim my forever with her, but it was no longer my forever to claim.

"I was so stupid to give into Brad."

Despite the years of bitterness I felt after learning of her involvement with my high school nemesis, I don't want her to beat herself up over me.

I shake my head. "Don't live with that regret. That's the past. Right?" Insecurity seeps into my words.

Her brows furrow. "Brad is the past I wish I never had."

Despite her answer, I can't shake the feeling that Liv will never want me as much as I want her. That someone else will come in and sweep her off her feet before I can lock her down.

Every night, I prayed for a miracle, or what I thought would be a miracle. For years, I asked God for another chance, and as much as those pictures of Olivia and Brad on social media poked holes in my hope, it never left. There was always a part of me that *knew* Olivia was meant to be mine. And in God's perfect timing, she's here with me once again. I just pray I won't mess up and ruin this second chance.

Olivia takes my hand and says, "Let's not focus on the past. Let's focus on the future, our future."

"That sounds good to me."

We talk for a few more moments, focusing on lighter topics, but when my phone doesn't stop buzzing with incoming texts and emails, I regretfully say, "I'm sorry, but I have some things that need my immediate attention."

She removes her hand from mine. "I am so sorry, I've been keeping you from your work. It still hasn't hit me that you own all of this."

"Me neither. Let me get yours and Dana's numbers so it's easier to track you down."

I hand her my phone and give her the code to unlock it.

She opens my contacts and adds in her number and then Dana's. Once she's finished she hands it back to me.

"I'll let you get back to work. I'm gonna go for a walk to explore this gorgeous beach up close. Can we talk more later?" she asks, looking shy.

"Of course." It's my turn to take her hand. Keeping my eyes locked on hers, I kiss her knuckles. "Enjoy your walk."

After texting Dana and asking for Liv's sizes, I send my assistant on a shopping run. Liv is going to be angry I'm not following her directions, but I have ten years to make up for and the time I finally get to have with her is priceless.

My security team confirms that Brad will be out on the next flight. I can breathe easier knowing he won't try to swoop in again. Apparently, he was the one who offered an obscene amount of money for the last-minute wedding. He thought he could win Liv back with a few slimy words. Thank the Lord, Liv saw through him.

As strong as she appears, I know deep down she's struggling. His betrayal is still fresh. My goal this week is to make her forget Brad Washburn even exists. I want to both take her back to where we first began and show her the future I ache to give her. The future I pray she wants, too.

TEN

Olivia

After Brad's departure and West's declaration, I go for a walk. West has work to do, and I have thoughts to work through.

Like, how my old best friend has become the most gorgeous billionaire I've ever laid eyes on. Not that I've ever met another billionaire.

West is absolute perfection. Not just his looks, but his heart. In high school, he stepped in to protect a girl he barely knew, despite the repercussions he'd have to face. Then he faced them and now lives with no regret.

During my prayer walk, I encounter several people who speak highly of him. West has built homes for the less fortunate and given them jobs all over the resort. He keeps their rent as low as possible and he pays them well to help them get back on their feet. The only part that surprises me about all of this is that he has the amount of money to make it all possible. It blows my mind.

He has always been a selfless soul, giving without reservation, even when it was all he had. Regret eats at me for not seeking him out after he left. But it hurt so much that he moved away without saying goodbye. The kiss he gave me was full of promise, but that promise felt empty when he left.

I can blame my dad for some of that hurt. It doesn't make sense that he handled things the way he did. But West was right; God's ways aren't always our ways. God's ways, even in the pain, are worth it. He works His good in His way and in His perfect timing.

Now West is back in my life, and my heart breaks at the thought of going back to my life without him.

You don't deserve any of this, my subconscious taunts me. *You moved on with Brad and almost married him despite still being in love with West. West deserves so much more than you.*

I pray the thoughts away and focus on the now. Now, I have West in my life, and he wants to take me on a date. With that thought, I head back to the penthouse to meet up with my sister and figure out how to navigate this life West flipped upside down in the best way.

Despite my request to keep it casual and not over-the-top, the moment I walk into my temporary home in West's penthouse, I find two rolling clothes racks. One is full of dresses; the other has more casual outfits. There's a long container full of shoes in a range of styles.

My eyes land on an envelope attached to the pole with my name written across the front in West's handwriting. I pull out the note.

My Dearest Olivia,

Here is an assortment of new clothes, including dresses for our upcoming dates. I know you don't want me to go over-the-top but when it comes to you, I can't help myself. Prepare to be spoiled. There are dresses, shorts, shirts, shoes, gowns, and everything in between. Wear whatever you like, even if it's jeans and a T-shirt. You look gorgeous in everything.

I can't wait to see you in the morning. I'll be there around 7.

Forever Yours,
West

I bite my lip and stifle a girly squeal when my sister walks in.

"Well, well, well, what do we have here?" she asks, thumbing through the designer gowns.

"A very rich West spending too much money on clothes." I tuck the note back into its envelope.

A slow smile spreads across her lips.

"Do you think he can buy me a new wardrobe next?" she asks, blinking her innocent eyes at me.

"Ask him yourself."

She shrugs as if it's something she'd be comfortable doing, then pulls out a white garment bag, leaving the hanger attached to the bar so she can unzip it. Inside is a gorgeous red gown.

Dana opens another garment bag, her mouth dropping open. "This is Dior." She proceeds to unzip several more bags, telling me the names of the luxury brands. There's Louis Vuitton, Gucci, Prada, and Versace.

I make her stop. "This is crazy."

My sister nods. "Yeah. He pulled out all the stops."

"When did he have time to do this?" I ask out loud, unzipping another bag that contains an emerald green dress. "These are incredible."

"And expensive," my sister muses. She shifts her gaze from the rack of clothes to me. "You better buckle up, buttercup, and enjoy this ride. Because sister Dana is going to live vicariously through you."

ELEVEN

Olivia

As we looked through the wardrobe West sent up, I told Dana all about the Brad drama. She never liked him and enjoyed the part about West forcing Brad to his knees to apologize to me. Even if his apology wasn't genuine. West bringing Brad to his knees was satisfying enough.

She slides on a cardigan and poses. "He had it coming. What he did to you was unforgivable."

"I don't want to hold on to it. Sure, I'm still angry and can't forgive him yet. But I will one day. I don't want my bitterness to taint the life God has given me."

"Which explains why God has given you a dreamy billion-aire," she says, bumping my shoulder with hers.

"There's something else," I say, my gut rolling at what I have to say next.

"What?"

"Do you remember the fire at the admin building back when I was in high school?"

Dana removes the cardigan and puts it back on the hanger, then locks her eyes on mine. "Yeah?"

"West thought he was responsible." Tears blur my vision.

"How?"

I tell her the rest of the story. By the time I'm finished, her eyes are misty.

"That's why he left?" She wipes at her eyes.

I nod. "Apparently, Dad wrote his family a letter stating if he and his parents left, he'd be free of any charges."

Dana launches herself at me and hugs me firmer than she's ever hugged me before.

"Dad has some things to answer for when we get home," she says as she pulls away.

"He does." My chest aches at the thought of going home, of leaving West.

I look through my new wardrobe to try to distract myself.

"So, what do you think of this?" I ask, holding up a powder blue sundress.

Dana's sad smile turns happy. "Perfect." She sorts through the shoes and pulls out white sandals "And these?"

"Love."

After hugging my sister good night, I head to bed. The mattress holds me just right. It's the perfect amount of soft and firm. West's room still smells of him. I sleep more peacefully than I have in ten years.

When I wake up, Dana curls my hair and I put on some tinted lip gloss, mascara, and a hint of blush.

At seven a.m. sharp, the bell dings.

"Coming!" Dana shouts before scrambling to the foyer and greeting West.

I follow behind, butterflies erupting in my midsection.

"Good morning," West greets Dana. When he sees me, he snaps his mouth closed. A muscle pulses in his jaw as he takes me in.

"Hi," I say, trying to break through the wave of nerves threatening to ruin this moment.

"You look stunning," West mutters, closing the distance between us in three long strides. The navy-blue suit, white button-down shirt, and no tie is slightly dressed down from the black suit he wore yesterday.

He takes my hands and twirls me. I can feel his eyes roam over me and don't hate the way it makes my insides turn gooey.

"Well, you two lovebirds have fun!" Dana says, grabbing her beach bag from the table and stepping into the elevator.

"Aren't we the ones leaving?" I ask West.

"Yes—" he begins.

Dana cuts him off. "But the helicopter pad is just above you." She squeals. "Can you believe it?" The door begins closing, so Dana adds, "Have fun!" before it shuts.

My gaze lands on West, whose eyes twinkle in amusement. "I thought I told you nothing over-the-top. A wardrobe of designer clothes was extravagant enough."

"Would you wear a designer dress to go on a mundane date?" he asks.

"To be honest, Mr. Lockwood, I've never worn a designer anything in my life. The closest I got was my wedding dress. And it pales in comparison to each of the outfits in those garment bags."

He looks nervous. "Is this too much for you?"

I motion to one of the outfits he bought me on a whim. "Yes."

He chuckles at my dramatics, but his expression sobers. "No, I mean going on a date with me. Since, you know, you were supposed to get married just a couple of days ago?"

"Reminders still sting, and I'm sure they will for a while. But seeing Brad and witnessing how he treats other people, I can't help but feel like I dodged a bullet. I think God has been nudging me for a while now. It's why I never got excited about planning. Even dress shopping was boring."

"Because God never wanted him for you."

I shrug, feeling stupid for spending so many years with that jerk. "The thought of breaking up with him made it feel like those five years were a waste of time. As if the years we dated were meaningless if we didn't get married."

"I can understand that." West is silent for a beat. "I don't want to push you into doing something you're uncomfortable with. Or something that feels too soon."

"This date isn't too soon. My breakup with Brad was five years too late." I never should have accepted his offer for the second date. In retrospect, I should have known he hadn't truly changed.

"You're sure then?" West's expression is hopeful.

"Definitely. So, who's flying the helicopter?"

A satisfied smile stretches across West's face. "One thing at a time." He takes my hand and kisses the back of it. "First things first. Breakfast."

"This is incredible!" I shout over the headset.

We are suspended from the clouds, hovering over a circle of waterfalls. They vary in height and width, all of them leading to a crystal-clear pool handcrafted by God. It's like looking at a little slice of paradise.

"This is something that makes me stand in awe of our Creator," West says over the headset. His voice is full of wonder and reverence.

Tears spring to my eyes. I fight the urge to take his hand.

"I was thinking the same thing," I respond.

After becoming a Christian, I knew I needed to marry a man who shared my faith. Brad went through the motions, attending church, listening to Christian music without complaint, and praying with me over meals. But that's where it all ended. For years, I settled. I don't know Brad's heart and I can't confirm or deny his salvation, but when I compare his proclaimed faith and actions to West's... there's no comparison. West pours into others while Brad only pours into himself.

I always had to remind Brad to pray before meals. West prayed over our food with sincerity and pure gratitude. Then he prayed over me and our time together. I didn't have to say a word. West took the initiative to put Jesus at the center of our day, and told me he wants Jesus at the center of our relationship, however it may unfold.

After a delicious breakfast on the roof with all my favorite breakfast foods, West helped me into his helicopter and we flew around the island where he pointed out landmarks, swimming locations, and things to do outside of the resort. Apparently, there's a gulf where the dolphins come in and allow you to swim with them. It's a well-kept secret, since it's West's land surrounding it, but he's swam with them a time or two.

Despite his immense wealth, West is humble and kind. If people treated others the way West treats strangers, the world would be a much better place.

He is so much more than I ever hoped for. Even more than I prayed for.

West sneaks a glance over at me and smiles. Its warmth floods me and thaws the places left frozen by Brad's betrayal.

"I knew you'd love it."

"Do you want a closer look?" he asks.

It's in this moment that I feel closest to God, not just because I'm seeing one of His many wonders before my eyes, but because He's working out His good for me despite my years of disobedience.

The water sparkles in the sunlight, somehow even more breathtaking.

"Oh my goodness, I don't know if I've ever seen something so beautiful," I whisper so low I doubt West can hear me.

"Neither have I," he says.

When I turn to look at him, his eyes are on me.

"So, what are we doing today?" Dana asks, then takes a bite of strawberry from her parfait.

"I don't know. West hasn't given me a hint about today's activity. Just that we need our swimsuits."

Dana taps her spoon against her lips as if she's deep in thought. "Hmm, I wonder."

Before I can ask her what she wonders, the familiar chime of the elevator fills the space and I jump up to greet West.

"Hey you," he says, strolling forward and wrapping me firmly in his arms.

"Hey." I look up at him and he presses a kiss to my forehead.

"What are we doing today that made you want to bring Dana?" I ask, narrowing my eyes playfully.

He pulls back, his arms still firmly around me. "Do you want to keep me all to yourself?"

My cheeks heat. Part of me does want to keep West all to myself, but he told me this activity is something he doesn't want my sister to miss out on. That thought warms me from my head down to my toes. He's always had a soft spot for Dana. Anytime we went to the neighborhood pool or splash park, he made sure he asked Dana if she wanted to go.

"Yes and no," I answer honestly. I play with the collar of his Hawaiian button down, a shirt that only he can pull off. "This week has been—" I look up at him, trying and failing to find the right word.

"Incredible, amazing, perfect?"

I smile, feeling the tension ease slightly. "Thinking rather highly of yourself?"

It's refreshing to see a confident West. He was always shy and unsure of himself in high school. I knew he could do great things. He was smart and ambitious, but his teenage insecurity held him back from trying anything beyond skateboarding and the drum line—not that being a drum major was anything to sneeze at.

"Anytime I see you smile and know I'm part of the reason for it, I think it's incredible, amazing, and perfect. Just like you." He leans forward, and one hand slowly skims up my spine, sending chills skittering across my skin. His touch lights me up and my heart rate kicks into overdrive. West's blue eyes are unhidden beneath his usual sophisticated glasses, and they darken as the distance between our lips grows shorter. Just when his lips are about to brush mine, my sister's voice rings through the moment, making West and I jump apart.

Dana has a mischievous smile. "Oops, sorry. Are we ready to go, though?" she asks, bouncing on her heels.

West looks at his watch. "Yes, I think it's about that time."

"Time for what?" I ask, trying to get a hint.

"Nice try, Livvy, but I'm not falling for that."

I pout and give him my best puppy dog eyes. It never failed me before with him. His face softens, but he shakes his head.

"You don't play fair." He grabs my hand and laces our fingers together.

Dana walks into the elevator first and taps her foot impatiently.

"Just know we're checking something off your bucket list," he says.

"That doesn't narrow it down much," I say, staring at his lips, feeling ready to burn my bucket list if it I means I can kiss him again.

Woah, girl. Calm down.

"Patience, love." He kisses my forehead again and I melt at his touch.

"Love?" I ask, my voice a breathy whisper.

His lips tilt up in a lopsided smile. "Too soon?"

There's not an ounce of doubt about how I feel about West. So, I shake my head and he smiles.

He releases my hand to wrap his arm around my back and gently brushes his fingers against my bare skin. "We won't rush this, but I can't hold back when it comes to you."

My heart does a double back flip, but when Dana clears her throat, I'm reminded that my sister is within earshot.

The three of us load into the fancy ATV parked in his private lot. I sit in the front with West and Dana sits in the back with our bags. We drive down the beach but have to duck into the woods for a bit before it opens back up to the gulf of Amber Island.

I hear the splashes before I see the dolphins leaping through the water and putting on the aquatic performance of a lifetime.

Dana claps and jumps out of the ATV the moment West parks under a group of palm trees.

"Dolphins!" She points at the mammals leaping through the air and pounds her feet like she's a toddler who's had too much sugar.

Before I have a moment to prepare myself, West pulls his shirt up and over his head, revealing a set of abs that would put Hercules to shame. My breath halts and my eyes take on a mind of their own as I absorb the majestic sight before me.

West crosses his arms over his chest and his muscles flexing does something to my insides, stirring to life something new and primal. Suddenly, insecurity tears me down. I've never been one of the skinny girls. Even in high school, I looked different from the other cheerleaders. But I didn't become insecure about it until Brad and I started dating. He always had something to say about my figure, and his eyes wandered to other women who – I couldn't help but notice – were thinner than me. Over time, an insecurity grew, and as much as I hate it, I can't shake it.

Dana is already walking into the water in her bikini, her clothes shed somewhere on the shore, unable to hide her excitement about swimming with the mammals.

West must see the look on my face, because his smile falls, and he walks to me with purpose.

"What's wrong?" he asks, brushing a hand down my arm.

"Look at you." I motion to him and his perfection. "You look like… like…"

"Something straight out of Greek mythology," my sister shouts. That girl must have ears as sharp as an elephant's.

West rolls his eyes.

"I didn't realize you'd be seeing me in my swimsuit. Like, I knew you would, but it didn't really hit me until now."

"I promise to keep my hands to myself." His gaze leaves a tingling warmth as it slides down me. I don't need to see his eyes that are hidden behind his dark sunglasses; I can *feel* them.

"Keeping your hands to yourself won't be a problem when you see me."

He furrows his brow. "What do you mean?"

"I don't look like a cover model for *Fitness Weekly*. I'm more like a popped open can of biscuits."

West doesn't mask his laugh but when he sees I'm not joking, he leans forward, sliding his sunglasses on top of his head, as if he wants me to see the sincerity in his eyes. "You are perfect exactly as you are. I spent my entire morning devotional asking the Holy Spirit to give me perseverance through today because I knew seeing you in a swimsuit would…" He trails off as his eyes drift down my body and snap back to my face. "You are too beautiful." He drops his sunglasses back into place.

"Close your eyes," I command.

"What?" he asks.

"Close your eyes and turn around so I can get in the water. I can't get in knowing you're watching me."

He pulls down his aviators, his blue eyes flashing in defiance. My heart skips a beat. His eyes have always been my greatest weakness.

"It's the only way I'll do it."

Finally, he relents and turns away from me. "Fine. But I want it on the record that I don't like it."

I quickly shed my T-shirt and shorts. After kicking off my sandals, I sprint toward the water and meet up with my sister, who is already shoulder deep.

The dolphins are about twenty yards out and have made no moves to leave anytime soon.

I feel West's chest press against my back. Apparently, I've been too absorbed in watching my favorite animal play in the water and didn't hear him get in.

He leans closer and his breath in my ear weakens my knees. "You are the woman of my dreams, exactly as you are. Never forget that." His arm wraps around me and he pulls me against his firm body. "There's not a thing I'd change."

His words heat me, their sincerity shining through each syllable. So much so that I start to believe him.

After pressing a kiss to my cheek, he tells me to cover my ears. I do as he says, then he whistles, the sound muffled yet shrill as he calls the dolphins in closer.

I remove my hands from my ears. "They follow your commands?" I ask, not hiding my surprise.

"I may have downplayed my involvement with this crew." He runs a hand through his hair, mussing the usual neat style. "We've spent quite a few days together."

"Obviously." I playfully roll my eyes and he smirks.

West releases me and swims out closer to the pod. His arms flex and his back muscles ripple with each stroke.

"Where can I get one of those?" Dana asks in a dreamy tone.

Irrational jealousy flares.

"I don't know, but you can't have mine."

She shoves my shoulder. "You never were good at sharing. Not that it matters in this case. That man only has eyes for you."

We spend the next hour swimming and playing with the dolphins.

West fulfilled one of my lifelong dreams today. Years ago, I told him about my silly fantasy to swim with dolphins. But not dolphins in a zoo or an aquarium — wild dolphins in the sea. West made it possible.

This week has been the absolute best week of my life. We went scuba diving on the coral reefs. Dined on his yacht, miles away from land. From morning until night, he's shared this life with me. He's even made sure Dana is entertained since he's monopolized all of my time – not that I'm complaining. After she eats breakfast with us, she has some sort of treatment done at the spa, plays tennis with other tourists, complete with her own private instructor – who I suspect she is secretly crushing on.

West has spared no expense, luxury, or thought when it comes to me. If he's trying to make up for the past, it's done. He has more than made up for leaving.

He's given me the world… while I've given him nothing.

TWELVE

West

My phone vibrates with an incoming call as I pull the ATV into its parking spot. I clench my jaw when I see the name on the caller ID. I excuse myself from Olivia and Dana to answer it.

"What's wrong?" Olivia asks after I hang up and return.

I run my hand through my hair. "The owner of Lucky Palms wants to have dinner tonight."

Olivia's face falls, but she quickly tries to mask it with a smile. "That's okay. I know you still have a business to run. Me and Dana will manage."

"I don't want to go," I tell her.

"Then don't," Dana adds nonchalantly.

Olivia swats her sister's arm. "West has things he needs to do. We don't need to make him feel guilty for living his life." There's something off about her tone and it sets me on edge.

"Come with me." It's more of a command than a request.

"Go with you to your business dinner? Won't that look unprofessional?" she asks.

"Not at all." I tug her closer. "It'll get this meeting over with, and I'll be able to do it with you beside me."

She bites her lip. "Okay, fine. But if this could end up hurting you or your business in any way…"

I tuck a loose strand of hair behind her ear. "If it ends badly for me but I still have you, none of that matters."

I brush my thumb against the edge of her jaw. As I lean forward, her eyelids flutter closed, but before I can brush my lips against hers, someone coughs.

"Dana?" a man asks.

Dana must spot Rhett, my lead tennis instructor, because she waves at him enthusiastically. He comes over to the three of us, looking more nervous than I've ever seen him. After greeting all of us, he focuses back on Dana.

"Do you have dinner plans tonight?"

"Not anymore." Dana spears me with a look.

"Want to have dinner with me?" he asks, taking her elbow and leading her away from me and Olivia.

She bounces on her toes and plays with the end of her braid as they talk, giving Olivia and me the opportunity to discuss our own plans.

"I'll pick you up in an hour."

"Okay." Olivia looks apprehensive. "What should I wear?"

I shrug. Giselle is always dressed to the nines, but that's because she's constantly on the prowl for husband number six.

"Wear whatever you want."

She purses her lips and gives me a sharp look. "What are you wearing?"

I cough and tug my shirt collar away from my neck. "Probably a black suit."

"So I need a fancy dress. Got it." She lifts a brow. "At least someone gave me an entire wardrobe of dresses recently."

"He must be smitten with you," I say.

She gives me a sly smile. "It's a good thing I'm smitten with him, too."

I walk into the penthouse and hear bumps and grumbles from somewhere inside.

"Olivia, are you ready?" I call, not wanting to infringe on her privacy.

"In here!" Dana calls from the direction of the master bathroom.

Olivia walks out in a deep purple dress that hugs each of her curves.

"You look beautiful." I take her hand and kiss her palm.

"You look very handsome," Olivia replies with a shy smile.

"You kids have fun!" Dana says before shuffling out of the bathroom and heading toward the elevator. "I'm meeting Rhett in a few minutes."

"Have fun and be good!" Olivia calls after her sister.

"Okay, Mom!" Dana shouts back.

Olivia and I head downstairs and take the town car to the restaurant just down the road. When we walk in, Giselle is seated and perusing the menu.

She smiles when she sees me, but her eyes narrow as she notices Olivia's hand on my arm. Olivia stiffens beside me.

"Weston!" she says when we reach her, then stands and kisses both of my cheeks.

I pull back and cough uncomfortably. "This is Olivia Swann, my..." I pause, looking over at Olivia and trying to decide on the best word to use. "Date." It doesn't feel like a strong enough description, but it will have to do for now. As much as I'd love to call Olivia mine, we are still on new ground and I want us to have that talk before putting a label on our relationship.

"It's a pleasure." Giselle extends her hand for Olivia to take.

Olivia shakes it awkwardly and sends me a sideways glance, looking incredibly uneasy. I give her my most reassuring smile and the tension appears to leave her shoulders.

"Nice to meet you," Olivia says.

After we order, the three of us fall into conversation. Giselle talks a lot about meeting me when I first came to the island and some of the funny times we shared. Olivia listens intently, smiling and laughing when appropriate.

As the evening goes on, Giselle and I talk more business. I ask Olivia her opinion on several things, and she gives me thoughtful answers. She doesn't realize it, but my goal is to one day soon have her name next to mine. Maybe I'm jumping the gun, but I've never been more sure about anything in my life.

When Olivia comes back from a trip to the restroom, she wears a look I can't quite decipher. All I know is that I don't like it.

She zones out while Giselle and I finish up our discussion. I try to hurry it along as quickly as possible because as time ticks on, Olivia becomes more and more tense.

Overall, this hasn't been an unpleasant dinner, but I'd rather have spent this time with Olivia one on one. Giselle isn't bad company, but I've always found her to be too flirty for my comfort.

When the waiter asks if we want dessert, I order mine and Olivia's to go.

We say goodbye to Giselle, and I take Olivia to the nearest park and we sit on a bench.

"I'm sorry. That was probably painful for you," I say, trying to ease the tension.

"Not at all. Giselle is a very impressive woman." Olivia swirls her spoon around the icing on her cake but never lifts it to her lips.

"I guess so."

"She's very beautiful. Built like a supermodel."

"She was a supermodel." The second the words leave my mouth, I want to take them back.

Olivia lifts a shoulder. "Not surprising."

I successfully burned the conversation to ash, so I sit and take a few bites of my chocolate cake.

"How's your cake?" I ask.

She lifts the tiniest amount to her mouth. The light in her eyes flickers, then immediately dims.

"I'm not really a dessert person." She puts the spoon back in the container.

I don't remind her that back in high school she'd often eat dessert before dinner.

"Is there anything you want to do before we go back?" I ask, attempting to save what's left of this evening.

In less than forty-eight hours, her plane will take her back to her life in Emerald Springs without me. And in these last four hours, she has built a wall high around her heart.

She shakes her head. "No, I'm getting really tired. This has been a busy week."

My heart sinks.

"I hope it's been a good one," I say, not hiding the desperation in my voice.

"The best." She smiles and an ounce of tension leaves me.

Something's still off, but I can't place it. To an outsider looking in, she looks content, but I see the insecurity creeping in. And I'm not sure how to stop it from taking complete control.

I quickly finish my dessert and close up hers for later.

On the short drive back, she falls asleep on my shoulder. Not wanting to disturb her, I carry her from the car to the elevator. When we reach the top floor, I carry her out to my bedroom where she's been staying. She's still in her dress and shoes. I tug off both shoes, turn the bed down, and tuck her in.

Before leaving, I kiss her forehead and whisper, "Sleep well, my love."

THIRTEEN

West

Pounding on my door wakes me from a restless sleep. When I open it, it's my most high-strung manager telling me about the cluster of problems that hatched overnight. Apparently, several sinks have sprung leaks, a snake is in the pool, and several of our shorter palm trees were tp'ed. We haven't had this many issues at once in years.

After grabbing a quick shower in my temporary apartment bathroom – that thankfully doesn't leak – I get on the phone with the plumbing company and confirm that they have several plumbers on their way. I head over to the entrance and ask security to pull the tapes to figure out who is responsible for this juvenile prank involving the palm trees.

Since they have the tp take-down under control, I head to the pool. The lifeguard is struggling to get the snake out and as much as I'd rather call animal control, I take the pole from him and do it myself. After disposing of the snake in the woods far enough away from the resort, I head back to my office to take a breath and check up on the other mundane issues that have popped up.

Someone knocks on my office door.

"Come in," I say, not looking up from my computer.

"I thought you should know your penthouse is clean and ready for you."

"What?" My head snaps up from the computer so fast I jar my neck. "Where's Olivia and Dana? They had more time here."

My assistant stares at me wide-eyed, clearly terrified to answer my question.

"They took the red eye to Emerald Springs." She pauses and looks away. They were scheduled to return on my jet. But Olivia probably knew I wouldn't approve of her abrupt departure. I pound my fist against my desk and rattle the figurines I've collected over the years. I texted Olivia last night that our time together would be delayed until after lunch. Despite having a great management team, I want to be a hands-on owner who gives his business the time and energy it requires.

Olivia took that opportunity to slip away.

"Why would she leave?" I ask rhetorically.

My assistant answers anyway. "She didn't say. Dana is the one who checked them out. Olivia was in the taxi before I could ask her."

"Thanks for letting me know." I dismiss my assistant and struggle to gather whatever composure I have left.

I slide my glasses off my nose, bury my hands in my hair, and hang my head.

After taking some time to gather myself, I call her and she doesn't answer, so I leave a voice message. I wait impatiently for an hour before sending her a text. No response.

> Please call me, Livvy.
>
> Tell me what's going on.
>
> We'll work through whatever this is together.

...

Hope flares in my chest, then vanishes the moment the text bubble disappears.

Having Olivia back in my life was a literal dream come true. I spent every possible moment praising God for my answered prayer.

Each day we spent together cemented my belief that Olivia was made to be mine, and I was made to be hers.

No one else on God's green earth is more perfect for me than Olivia Swann. I thought I proved that to her this week. I thought I showed her in my words and actions how much I want her, how deeply I love her.

But like I've always feared, she doesn't want me. I'll never be enough for her.

Olivia

I had to leave. I had to get away and let West live the life he deserves. Because he deserves so much more than me.

When we were at dinner and I went to the restroom, I overheard some waitresses talking. They couldn't believe I was West's date and not Giselle. They confirmed my insecurity that Giselle would be a much better match for West. She's gorgeous, kind, and ambitious. Just like him.

Giselle took every chance available to touch West. His arm, his shoulder, even on a couple of wildly inappropriate occasions, his face. Giselle made it crystal clear that she wasn't going to let West be with another woman without a fight. I'm not sure if they ever dated, but if the way her gaze lingered on him when she thought I wasn't looking was any indication, I'd say Giselle is in love with him.

Giving him a chance with Giselle goes against my heart's every desire, but it has to be done. She's the woman he deserves. Not me.

When I got home, I discovered Brad had thrown all my belongings into mine and Dana's apartment. Which was an odd relief. He left his key with the front desk, but I didn't trust that he didn't make copies, so we changed our locks. Thank the good Lord I haven't heard from him since Amber Island.

Every day I go to work, come home, and try to write. I thought since I experienced double heartbreak in the span of a week, I could throw all that emotion into a novel. But I haven't finished a single one. Not even the new ones. I still nail the dark moments where the couple fights, separates, and struggles with their broken emotions, but when I reach the part where the couple is supposed to get their happily ever after, writer's block slams into me.

No matter how many walks I go on, no matter how many Pinterest boards I make that have images of happy couples, I can't give my characters the happily ever after they've fought tooth and nail to achieve.

I've come to a depressing and powerful realization: I'm no author. I'm a failure. As a writer. As a fiancée. As an almost girlfriend. As a friend.

Dana barges into my room without knocking. If it wasn't for the door stopper, she would have punched the handle right into the wall.

"What are you doing? Still moping and being downright stupid?"

"Excuse me?!" I ask, standing up from my desk where I've been staring blankly at one of my many incomplete manuscripts.

"Liv. West is still very clearly in love with you. Why would you run away from that?" Her eyes glisten with tears. "Don't you realize there are people close to you who wish a man would love them the way West loves you? How can you be so selfish?"

My sister is clearly dealing with her own heartbreak, but I can't bring myself to sympathize with her right now. Something happened with Rhett, but she hasn't said a word until now, and I've been too focused on my own issues to get to the bottom of her heartache.

"I'm trying to be selfless!" I exclaim, not caring if our neighbors can hear me. "West is too good for me. I don't deserve him."

Dana settles her hands over her hips. "When are you going to get it through your thick skull? God gives us more than we deserve. It's called grace, Olivia. G-R-A-C-E." She spells it out. "We don't deserve our next breaths. We don't deserve a single good thing God gives us. But He gives it to us, anyway."

Her words sink in. Then I see the tears spilling down her cheeks. "We don't always understand His ways. A lot of times, the paths He sets us on are hard and test us. But they're designed to bring us closer to Him." She wipes the tears from her cheeks.

My heart softens toward her. "You're on your own heartbreak path, aren't you?"

She throws her hands up and drops them. "Yes. It's stupid." After she tosses herself onto my bed, I lay down beside her and take her hand.

I've been so caught up in myself, I selfishly ignored my sister's silent pleas for companionship and empathy. When I turn my head to face her, I ask, "What happened?"

She releases a deep sigh. "We had an amazing date the night we left. I texted him while we were on the plane to tell him we were leaving and that I really wanted to keep in touch, but I got a response from his phone carrier saying his phone number was no longer in service."

"Are you sure you had the right number?"

"We had texted a little before our date, so yes, I had the right number." She turns her head away from me. "He ghosted me."

I sit up and pull her up to sit next to me. She still refuses to face me.

"Listen here." I shake her arm. "If he ghosted you, he's not worth it. Don't let him settle in a single one of your brilliant brain cells."

Her shoulders shake with a laugh before she turns and faces me. Her eyes are rimmed in red. "You think I have brilliant brain cells?"

I crack a smile. "I thought they were the most brilliant until this."

Dana narrows her eyes. "What do you mean?"

"You've allowed a man you spent a week with to break your heart." I raise a brow.

"And you walked away from a man who is head over heels in love with you because you don't see your own worth." She stands up.

"It's not that I don't think—"

"When was the last time you read your Bible?"

My nostrils flare as I stare my younger sister down. But she doesn't retreat or look one bit intimidated.

Finally, I relent. "On the plane."

"That was a month ago. You haven't been to church or Bible study either. Stop taking out your frustrations on Jesus. He's calling for you. His arms are open and He wants you to follow His will."

"And you know what His will is?" I ask, my voice rising in frustration.

"I can't say for certain. But I believe the reason you've failed to finish a manuscript, the reason why you've been holed up in your bedroom for weeks, the reason you've been down-right miserable to be around, is because you're running from Him, from His will, and His blessing: Weston Lockwood."

"What about you?" I ask.

"What about me?"

"Are you going to stay heartbroken over a stupid man who ghosted you?"

"No." She straightens to her full height and raises her chin. "But I am going to make sure that you don't miss out on the blessing God has given you."

I let go of the unfair anger I have toward my sister and wrap my arms around her. "Thanks for always looking out for me. I'm sorry for lashing out at you."

She pulls back. "You don't need to apologize. I know you're hurting. Which is why I want to fix this."

FOURTEEN

West

I wanted to give Olivia the time she needed to work through everything. But with all of my text messages unanswered and none of my phone calls returned, I am struggling to keep myself in Amber Island.

Olivia's life was shaken up when Brad cheated. But when she arrived here and realized who I was, she seemed excited. Maybe that was my overactive imagination conjuring what I've been hoping for the last ten years.

I've been contemplating going back to Emerald Springs and reconnecting with my old neighbors as an excuse to find her and beg her to forgive me for whatever it is I messed up. I knew she was uncomfortable around Giselle and have kicked myself a dozen times for not pushing my dinner with Giselle back a week or two. Nothing we discussed was "pressing," as she had originally stated.

Something was off with Olivia that night, and I knew it. Despite her falling asleep on me, there was a barrier between us. The following day, I planned on tearing it down and telling her exactly what my intentions were. But she never gave me that chance. Instead, she ran.

Just like you did.

During every date, we had easy conversations. She caught me up on her life and even told me a little about the books she was working on. Everything with her felt as natural as breathing. I actually breathed easier having her with me. Now it feels like I'm running out of air.

As I pace my living room, going over every moment we spent together that week, the ding of the elevator fills my home's emptiness.

I check my watch, wondering if it's the food delivery service with my lunch. But they'd be too early and they always check in with the front desk, who buzzes me first.

I practically run to the foyer and as the elevator doors open, a whoosh of cleansing air fills me as Olivia's beautiful face comes into view. She's wearing a teal dress that's so long it almost brushes the floor. A sunhat covers her sugar brown hair and her eyes are full of regret.

"Olivia?" I don't mask the emotion in my voice.

"Hi," she says, as if she didn't break my heart a mere month ago.

"What are you doing here?"

She licks her lips and I can't help the memories that surface of us as teenagers in the hallway where I attempted to convey everything I've ever felt for her into a single kiss.

After a deep breath, she says, "I'm sorry."

My mind is at war with my heart. I stare at her in silence before I finally break. "You're sorry? You walk out of my life with no warning and all you have to say is you're sorry?" I wince at my words but I can't take them back.

"Believe me when I say I know how bad it hurts." There's not an ounce of hostility in her voice; instead, the sincerity of her words shines through. "I am sorry. So sorry. I needed time to breathe and work through the emotions I thought I had buried a long time ago."

"We could have worked them out together," I say, attempting to conceal my frustration.

"I'm sorry, West. I never meant to hurt you. When I ran, I thought I was protecting myself from getting hurt again. The truth is, I only hurt myself."

"And me."

"And you. And you are the last person I wanted to hurt. I'm so sorry about that." She looks down and her tears splash onto my floor. "That entire week was amazing, and you made me feel so... treasured. But then when we had dinner with Giselle, I overheard the waitresses talking when I went to the bathroom about how you and Giselle would be perfect together and all my insecurities came to a head. It didn't help that she touched you every chance she got."

A growl comes unbidden from the back of my throat. "I need to have a talk with her about that. She's always been touchy, but I only want one woman's hands on me." I take Olivia's hands in mine and rest them on my chest, hoping she feels the erratic beat of my heart. A heart that beats for her alone.

Heat sparks in Olivia's eyes but soon vanishes. She shakes her head and her hands drop to her sides. "One of the waitresses couldn't believe I was your date over Giselle, the retired model, especially since I was such a 'mousy girl.'" Olivia puts "that mousy girl," in finger quotes.

I grip both of her shoulders. The need to touch her, hold her, kiss her, is growing into a painful desperation. "Mousy? Did they really use that word? Because you're not mousy!"

"Be serious, West. If you were honest with yourself, what would be your type?" She steps out of my hold and I hate the space separating us.

"My type?" I ask, feeling slightly unhinged. "My type is Olivia Swann. That's it." I slice my hands through the air, attempting to make my point.

"I'm not a type, West. I'm not any man's type."

"Good. You're not supposed to be any man's type. You're my type. *Mine*." She sucks in a sharp breath, staring at me wide-eyed. Before getting my hopes up, I ask, "Are you going to run again?"

She shakes her head. "No. I'm not planning on it. I'm here to stay. Well, not here, in your penthouse, but on your island."

"You are?"

"If that's okay with you?"

Emotions battle within me. Apprehension, excitement, fear. When I say nothing, her face falls. She's undoubtedly assuming the worst.

Looking at the floor, she whispers, "If it's not, then I'll go back to Emerald Springs and never bother you again." Olivia looks up at me and everything inside of me tightens at the vulnerability written across every inch of her gorgeous face.

"You could never bother me, Livvy." Her eyes sparkle when I use my old nickname for her. "This last month without you did bother me, though. I thought I came on too strong. That the dates were too much. That—"

"You thought I left you because I didn't want you?" she asks.

"Exactly."

"Believe me when I say I've wanted you from the moment I saw you. But I never felt like I was good enough for you."

Anger fills me. "Why would you *ever* think that?"

"That week, you exceeded any woman's wildest dreams. And what did I give you?"

"You. You gave me you. Which is all I need in this life. And Lord willing, I'll have you in the next life too." I spread my arms open, trying to emphasize our surroundings. "God has given me all of this, and I thought you coming back into my life was His way of showing me who to share it with. But Livvy, you took my heart with you when you left."

"I'm so sorry. I never wanted to hurt you. I wanted to set you free to be with someone who doesn't hold you back. Who matches your attractiveness, ambition, and success." She looks at the floor and mumbles, "Someone like Giselle."

I don't even want to acknowledge her assumption about Giselle. "You have been my fantasy since I was fifteen years old. No one else matches me like you do. Freedom for me is with you, not without you."

She looks back up at me. "Do you really mean that?" Her voice is barely a whisper.

I take a step forward, tucking my hands into my pockets to keep myself from touching her. "Yes. With every ounce of my existence, I mean that."

"Then when you left Emerald Springs, when you left me, why didn't you say goodbye?" she asks and her question tears me apart.

"The same reason you didn't when you left."

Silence stretches.

"It'd be too hard," she answers. "I get it now but... You took the best parts of me when you left." Tears roll down her cheeks. "I wanted to forget about it. I wanted to forget about you. But that day... in the hallway. My back pressed against the lockers, your mouth on mine, the passion in your kiss. The way my lips tingled long after you walked away... I'd never be able to forget you."

Despite the seriousness of this moment, I smirk. "That was the point."

She shakes her head and bites her lip. I reach forward and gently pull her into my arms.

Without overthinking it, I lean forward and claim her lips like I've dreamt of doing for the last ten years. No woman has ever come close to Olivia in my eyes. Not their beauty, not their kindness, not their anything. Because if I've learned anything through these trials, it's that God has a plan in everything. Even when we make mistakes, stumble, or fall. When we're at our weakest, He pulls through and reveals His strength. He had to be my strength when she left. Leaving her ten years ago was hard enough, but having her leave me without a goodbye was excruciating.

I pour all my promises into the kiss, allowing it to soothe the marks she left on my heart. Allowing it to carve out my regrets and everything that's tarnished our relationship. She kisses me back with fervor, filling the empty spaces and healing the parts of me she broke when she left. As she presses herself into me, I'm reminded of how perfectly she fits me. Not just physically, but emotionally.

I pull back and allow us both a moment to breathe.

"I love you, Olivia Swann. I've loved you for a long time, and I've prayed for you twice as long. You started off as my best friend and there's no doubt in my mind that God made you for me and had His hand in this all along. Even in the separations."

There's another ding as the elevator doors open and Dana peeks her head out. Olivia takes a step away from me.

"I was a part of this too!" Dana says. "I helped be a bridge with both separations. So you can thank me now."

"You've kept yourself shut in there?" I ask.

"I knew you and Olivia needed a moment of privacy, but it gets stuffy in there." Dana fans herself.

"You're right, I never thanked you. If it wasn't for you, I don't know if this ever would have worked. So, thank you."

Dana beams at me. "It was my pleasure."

The three of us cook dinner together and eat out on the patio. We talk and laugh as if no time or distance has ever come between us.

Olivia's phone rings and when she glances at the screen, she winces.

"Who is it?" Dana asks, looking over the table at it.

"Dad." Olivia glances up at me. "It's a FaceTime call."

My spine stiffens. I stand and pick up our dishes, depositing them on the counter to wash later. When I step back onto the porch, Olivia and Dana have their faces squished together to both fit on the screen.

I cross my arms and lean against the doorway, amused by how these two sisters could be so similar yet so different.

Without warning, they turn the phone on me.

I stand at attention the moment my eyes collide with Mr. Swann's.

I cough, feeling every part the awkward teenager I was when I left Emerald Springs after receiving Mr. Swann's letter.

"Hello, Mr. Swann."

"West, it's good to see you. I hope your mother and father are well." The formality of his tone does nothing to help my nerves.

"They are. Traveling through Spain right now."

"Good, good." Mr. Swann nods, his usual confidence appearing to fade. "Listen, I wanted to apologize for the confusion about the fire." His mustache twitches. "Liv told me you received a letter from the station with my signature."

"And the mayor's seal!" Dana pipes in.

"It wasn't from me. I don't make deals like that. That's not how those cases work."

"Then who would have done it?" I ask, then mutter, "Who had access to the mayor's seal other than the mayor?"

Olivia gasps. "Brad." She taps Dana's arm repeatedly.

"What?" Dana asks, brushing Olivia's hand away as if it's an irritating fly.

"Brad worked for the mayor that year. He did the filing and made coffee runs. I bet you he got a hold of it and faked it all."

Dana doesn't look convinced. "West and Brad had beef in high school, but it wouldn't be so serious that he'd frame West for something so awful." She tilts her head. "Unless…"

"Brad was the one who started the fire," Olivia says.

I nod. The football coach forbade anyone on the team to smoke. I saw Brad toss a cigarette into the trash can that day when he was meeting with a teacher about his grades, but I assumed he had put it out first. My assumption was clearly wrong, and I should have looked into it more, but after receiving the official letter, I forgot all about it.

"That's quite an accusation, Liv," Mr. Swann says.

"Brad smoked in high school. I saw him drop cigarettes into trash cans a few times and he didn't always make sure they were out. He avoided the admin building like the plague, so I never thought he was responsible. But that year, he was failing several classes so I bet he had to meet with those teachers outside of school hours instead of at their actual offices," Olivia says.

"I'll look into it. I'm not sure how far we'll get, but it would explain a lot." Mr. Swann's gaze shifts to me. "I'm sorry you've been dealing with the guilt all this time."

"It's water under the bridge." I pull Olivia over to me, wrapping my arm around her waist. Dana stands in front of us, holding the phone up so all three of us can fit on screen. Dana doesn't hide her irritation.

"Dad, my arm hurts and we've done enough of your investigative work for you. So we're gonna go."

Mr. Swann chuckles. "All right, sweethearts, I'll talk to you soon." He focuses on me. "You take care of my girls."

"Yes, sir."

After hanging up, Dana calls it a night.

Now that Mr. Swann has these facts, hopefully justice will be served. But none of us wants to revisit that right now. It's all in the past, as far as I'm concerned.

Dana gathers her things then we walk her to the foyer. She hugs her sister and me before leaving.

The moment the elevator doors close, I grab Olivia around the waist and pull her against me, claiming her mouth in a slow kiss.

"Ten years was a long time to be away from you," she says, pulling back just enough to wrap her arms around my neck.

"We have forever to go," I reply, holding her tight and thanking God for my priceless gift.

EPILOGUE

Olivia

One Year Later…

"Take off your sandals," my sister commands.

I do as she asks and pull off each one. "First you force me into this dress, then you blindfold me. What in tarnation is going on?"

"Have I ever steered you wrong?" she asks.

"Well, you steered me into that post two minutes ago. So, yes."

"Sorry again." I can sense her grimace even if I can't see it.

"I'll forgive you *if* you tell me where we're going."

"Just take a step forward."

The moment my toes hit the sand, several violins begin playing a beautiful melody that harmonizes with the crashing waves.

"What's going on?" My heart goes wild in my rib cage. West has been dropping hints left and right about proposing.

We've taken our relationship slowly. West didn't want to rush me into anything so soon after Brad's betrayal. But he made sure I knew he was courting me and not casually dating me. He wants to make me his wife. That's something he's made crystal clear from the very beginning of our new relationship.

Every night, we sit out on his balcony as the sun sets and talk about our past and our future. On several special occasions, he's read the prayers he prayed for me, which made me cry every single time. West's heart is the most beautiful thing in this world.

His beautiful heart and his selfless actions have given me an endless amount of happily forever afters for my characters. I could never complete a manuscript before now because I didn't know how to portray true love. The only love I experienced broke me. God used that brokenness to heal me, too, in the only way He can — unexpectedly and thoroughly.

Who knew my meddling sister would be a key component to bringing my love life full circle?

As my sister removes my blindfold, it pulls me back into this confusing and exciting moment.

My hands fly to my mouth when I see West kneeling at the center of a heart of candles and rose petals holding a small jewelry box.

There are five men in tuxedos playing the violin behind West. The song changes from something upbeat and catchy to low and moody.

He smiles at me and it takes me back to our days and nights together as two bright-eyed teenagers.

West doesn't give me a moment to speak — not that I even have words — before he begins his heartfelt speech.

"Olivia Robin Swann. You are the love of my life, the light in my eyes, and the steady beat of my heart. God gave me you when I was in my darkest place. You were the light that brought me through. Even before I understood the meaning of prayers, I thanked God for you. So today, I am asking you, Livvy, will you be mine forever?"

I glance around, taking in the effort and detail he put into this moment. Everything from the songs the violinists play, to the rose petals' shade of red, down to the gorgeous emerald-cut diamond ring in the jewelry box. But all of that pales in comparison to the man kneeling before me. West Lockwood, the boy I secretly crushed on years ago, is now the man I will spend my forever with.

"Yes!"

He carefully removes the ring from the box and slides it onto my finger. It's the perfect fit.

After West stands, I expect a kiss, but instead he leans forward and whispers, "Welcome to forever, my love."

Several flashes distract me as a photographer captures this moment in time. The violinists continue their song as West pulls me into his arms and we dance slowly in the candlelit heart on the beach.

West

As much as I hoped for it, my dreams could never compare to my reality. Olivia Swann, now Lockwood, is fast asleep on my chest. Her hair fans out behind her on the sheets and her pillow soft lips puff out with each exhale.

I stroke a finger down her cheek and stare at her in wonder. A year and a half ago, my prayers had turned desperate. When I saw her pictures with Brad, I thought she had forgotten about me. That somehow my memories were dreams and not reminders of times past.

She stirs and her eyes open slowly. The sun peeks through the curtains of our honeymoon suite and its rays dance across her face as she sits up.

"Good morning," she says, her voice coming out husky.

I trace my finger down her arm. "Good morning."

After placing an achingly slow kiss to my lips, she gets out of bed, wraps her robe around her shoulders, and finds the breakfast cart ready and waiting.

"I'm starving," she announces.

"Me too," I say, allowing my eyes to roam over my gorgeous wife.

She bites her lip, shakes her head, and pours us each a glass of freshly squeezed orange juice.

The kitchen loaded the cart with eggs, bacon, waffles, and a variety of fruits, including a strawberry, blueberry, and vanilla yogurt parfait, which she grabs. I follow her over and fill my plate with eggs, bacon, and a waffle, covering it with a healthy dose of syrup.

"Can we eat outside?" she asks.

"Whatever you want, my love."

There's a small table with two chairs that's perfect for breakfast in the morning and tea in the evening. The Eiffel Tower is just in the distance.

I pull her chair over so she'll be beside me and she sits. I take the spot next to her. After we send up a prayer of thanks, we both dig into our food.

"How do you stay so fit, eating like that?" She pokes my stomach.

"Exercise and only indulging on special occasions."

"Maybe you can help me with that now that we're married."

"Help you with what?"

"Losing weight."

I turn to face her and gently grip her face in my hands. "You are perfect exactly as you are."

Her eyes sparkle with unshed tears. "Somehow, you make me believe it."

"Because it's true." I lean over and press my lips against hers. I pour every ounce of desire I feel for her into our kiss. "Believe me now?"

She bites her lip. "I don't know. I think there's more you can do to prove it."

"Oh, I plan to, Mrs. Lockwood. But first, you need to eat."

We eat and discuss our plans for the rest of the day.

After taking our plates inside, I shut the French doors and settle my hands on her hips, pressing her back against the cool glass. Leaning forward, I claim her mouth in another kiss.

She's breathless when I finally pull away.

"I still can't believe you chose me." Before I have a moment to respond, she adds, "You could have any woman you want. Why me?"

"There would never be anyone else. You've been it from the very beginning. You're my forever, Olivia. I knew it at fifteen, and it was confirmed when you showed up at my resort. And you knew I was yours. Maybe you didn't realize who I was at first—"

She cuts me off. "But my heart did." This time, she kisses me. "And it always will."

BONUS EPILOGUE

Dana

As happy as I am for my sister and West, I've been asking God if I'll ever get my own happily ever after.

While Liv and West spend their honeymoon in Paris after their fairytale wedding, I'm stuck in a bungalow, alone. Technically, I'm not in my bungalow. I'm walking barefoot down the beach, the golden sand squishing between my toes, but still.

I *know* I'm being whiney while I live what would be a dream for other people, and I am grateful for this life. Truly, I am. But like West, I want someone to share this life with. Have children, a dog. Well, maybe I can get the dog on my own. But having another person to help with this imaginary dog would be nice. Having a husband to love and cherish me would be wonderful and, of course, I'd love and cherish him too.

Following God's will for my life has always been my goal. But since I was a little girl, my desire has been to be a wife and mom. If God planted that desire in my heart, then why hasn't He brought me my own Prince Charming?

No Prince Charming for me… I feel as though I'll be single forever.

Maybe forever is a *little* dramatic. But it just hit me today that I will no longer be living with my sister. She's going to be moving in with her billionaire Prince Charming once they return from their month-long honeymoon in the City of Love.

Bitterness envelops me as memories wash over me. It was stupid to believe, but I thought maybe, just maybe, Rhett would be my happily ever after. But the day after our first and only date, he vanished.

Rhett took ghosting someone to the next level. So much so that I had to ask my sister and West if Rhett even existed or if he was someone I dreamed up with my overactive and deeply desperate imagination.

We only had a handful of lessons and one date, but our conversations, laughs, and lingering touches have stayed with me. We spent our date night at a beautiful rustic restaurant right on the water. The weather was perfect. I thought the same about my company.

"You look beautiful," Rhett had said as his gaze raked over me. He pulled out my chair and I sat down.

"Thank you."

He made his way to his side of the table and took his seat. When he smiled at me, the faint lines around his eyes became more pronounced.

"I'm so happy to be here with you tonight." He reached across the table and without hesitation, I put my hand in his.

"Me too."

When the waiter came over to take our order, I expected Rhett to pull his hand back, but he didn't. Instead, he stroked my palm with the rough pad of his thumb, sending sparks up my arm.

Rhett motioned for me to order first, and he earned another point for the gentleman category. I ordered a chicken salad and he ordered a steak fajita.

I glanced down at our hands; his tan skin was a dark contrast to my pale tone. That's when I noticed his scars. The back of his hand was covered in white patches of skin, mostly over his knuckles. As much as I wanted to ask him about them, I didn't. That's not exactly a great ice breaker for a first date.

Instead, I said, "Thank you for keeping me busy when I probably would have gone stir crazy."

He lifted a dark eyebrow. "Oh, so now I'm just a distraction for you?" Rhett's lips tipped up in a teasing smile.

"A good distraction." I pursed my lips to the side, trying to come up with the best explanation. "A short, vacation fling."

Rhett released my hand and sat up straighter, all playfulness leaving his face. "You're not a fling for me, Dana Swann."

I lifted my hands in a placating gesture. "It was a joke. I'm not a fling kinda gal."

An awkward silence stretched between us. Unable to meet Rhett's eyes, I took my cloth napkin from the table and carefully placed it on my lap, paying way more attention and care to it than necessary.

"Good."

My eyes snapped up to meet his. His face was still all hard lines and a handsome kind of terrifying, but some of the tension that had descended over us lifted.

"If this isn't a fling for you, what made you want to go out with me?" I asked, folding my hands.

"Diving in headfirst, huh?" he asked, clearly amused. Any remaining tension vanished.

I shrugged. "I'm not a toe dipper." The words were out before I could think them through.

"A toe dipper?" He tried, and failed, to fight his laugh.

"Yeah, like you know people who go swimming and want to dip their toe in the water to see if it's too hot or cold before they get in?"

"I guess," he said as more of a question than a statement.

"Well, I've never been that way. There's no toe dipping, I'm either all in or I'm out. No matter the consequences. I'll either freeze or get burned. Risks make things more exciting."

"At the pool or in life?" he asked.

"Both."

Rhett stared at me, studying me as if he was picking through the various pieces of my brain and trying to figure out who I am. It made me squirm. I took several large gulps of water, my mouth suddenly parched.

"That's probably why I like you."

I blinked in surprise then narrowed my eyes. "I haven't figured out why I like you yet."

Rhett's confidence never wavered. "That's easy."

"Yeah?"

"I'm handsome, funny, charming, and you like how it feels when I'm pressed against you."

My cheeks burned and I immediately regretted taking another gulp of water because it got stuck in my throat and I drew the entire restaurant's attention with my coughing. Rhett came up behind me and gave my upper back a few hard pats, successfully clearing my airway and allowing me to breathe again. My eyes watered for several moments as I tried to gather any semblance of composure. He took his spot across from me once more.

"My joke was not meant to deliver such a literal punch."

We both laughed.

When the food arrived, he reached across the table again, this time taking both of my hands in his. He prayed over our food, the sincerity of his words overwhelming me. He was so genuine and so grateful.

I never imagined meeting a man as attractive and confident as Rhett who also had such a firm faith.

"How long have you been a Christian?" I asked, pouring the dressing over my salad.

"A few years. How about you?"

"How do you know I'm a Christian?"

He smirked and I noticed his slightly crooked front teeth. "Most people would say it's because of the cross you wear every day, and that's part of it, but it's how you treat others." Rhett took a bite of his fajita, a little sauce running down his chin that he quickly wiped away.

"How I treat others?" I picked through my salad and stabbed my favorite parts: the bacon pieces and hard-boiled egg.

"You're always smiling at people, even when they wear a permanent scowl. Mr. Roberts is the most miserable man I've ever met, yet you had him smiling on day one," Rhett said, referring to the old man who handed out towels outside the gym and tennis courts.

"Well, he's always been perfectly pleasant to me."

"Probably because you treat him the same way you treat everyone, with kindness and respect. Most guests treat him like a servant. Instead of letting him eat alone, you invited him to eat with you. I've never seen another guest do that."

Rhett was talking about the time I saw Mr. Roberts at lunch. He sat against the side of one building on the ground, eating a sandwich alone. I invited him to eat with me since I was also alone and genuinely wanted the company.

"That wasn't a big deal," I said, brushing off the compliment.

"Maybe not to you, but for him, it was huge."

I bit my lip. "My parents raised Olivia and me to respect all people, to treat others how they want to be treated. I don't like eating alone, so I thought maybe he felt the same way."

"Believe it or not, I've asked Mr. Roberts to eat with me a few times. He's always turned me down. But I'm convinced you can thaw the most frozen heart." He brushed his thumb against my cheek. "You've thawed me."

I melted right on the spot.

Rhett was a complete gentleman throughout the rest of the evening.

We talked more about our beliefs and values and eventually our conversation ventured onto our families.

"My brother was the golden child growing up," he said.

"Sounds like my sister."

"Don't get me wrong, I know Mom loved us all, but she always had a special place for Caleb. He was her first born and the apple of her eye. Caleb is the one who resembled our dad the most."

When he saw my look of confusion, he explained, "Dad died when I was just a kid. Caleb took on the role of dad and big brother since Mom had to double her shifts to afford life as a single parent."

Reaching across the table, I squeezed his hand. "I'm sorry to hear that. I don't know what I'd do if I lost my dad."

Rhett's gaze drifted to our hands. He laced his fingers through mine.

"You'd take it one day at a time. You'd do what needed to be done, because even though the world seems to stand still, it doesn't. It spins on and you have to move along with it."

He pulled his hand away and focused back on his fajita.

After several moments of tension-filled silence, he asked, "Do you ever fear you'll never be enough? That your sister will always be more than you are?"

I swallowed the last bite of my food. "Every day."

Anytime I've shared that tidbit about myself with anyone else — feeling inadequate — people have brushed me off and told me I was being ridiculous. That no one has ever compared me to Olivia and that they hold both of us Swann girls to a higher standard because of our fire chief father. That much is true. But I've never been as smart as Olivia, or as calm as Olivia.

"Your older sister was my favorite student. She always turned assignments in on time. She never gave me an issue in class. Why can't you be more like her?"

They're phrases I heard countless times through school.

Why can't I be more like Olivia? Because I was — I am — a different person than her.

What was amazing about Rhett was that his story mirrored my own. He opened up first, sharing those vulnerable pieces of himself. It made me feel safe to share the same.

He understood me in a way no one else has. I thought I understood him, too.

We discussed nothing else about our pasts. That was fine, because I'm all for living in the present. Which is why I hate that I can't get him — a man from my past — out of my head.

But the way he kissed me is permanently imprinted into every cell of my body.

When he dropped me off at the penthouse where Olivia and I were staying, he slowly leaned forward, making his intentions clear.

"I really want to kiss you, Dana." His breath smelled of spearmint from the gum he had chewed. His lips barely brushed mine as he added, "Pull away if you don't want this."

I didn't pull away, though. I leaned forward and every one of my senses came to life. One of his hands lazily made its way up my bare arm to cup the back of my neck. The other slid around my waist to my back as he deepened the kiss, curling my toes and making my heart slam like a sledgehammer. Chills and heat worked through me, cooling and heating me all at once. My nerve endings fired at lightning speed, making me dizzy, but I knew I was on solid ground. In a single kiss, Rhett became my solid ground.

He wished me a good night, and hours later, he was gone.

When Liv told me she wanted to leave that night, I sent him a text to let him know. But the response wasn't from him; it was from his phone carrier, informing me his number was no longer in service.

Which is why I had to double check with West that Rhett actually existed after Olivia and I returned to Amber Island. West confirmed that Rhett did in fact exist but quit his job through email. Rhett sent his resignation letter from an email address that no longer accepts messages. And with that, I lost any possibility of finding him.

How could a man kiss me like that and then never speak to me again?

It's been over a year and he has yet to reenter my life. Part of me wants to seek him out, but I don't know where to look. I feel pathetic that it still bothers me, but I thought we had a real connection.

He got me to open up by sharing his vulnerabilities. I thought that meant something. I thought *I* meant something to him. But I didn't. It was just a date, and I was just another woman, despite his assurances that I wasn't a fling.

I held out hope that maybe God has the same or a similar plan for me as He did for Olivia and West. But after West told me Rhett quit without notice, I knew my hope was pointless. Rhett was a mistake. I didn't know him long enough to suffer a broken heart from his abandonment, but he left a fracture behind. A fracture that refuses to heal.

That amazing, mind numbing, heart thumping, time jumping kiss was his goodbye kiss.

My spiraling thoughts are interrupted when I almost trip over a body on the beach. And not just a fish or whale washed up on shore, but a human body.

A HUMAN BODY!

All my limbs seize, my blood runs cold, and I'm frozen to the spot as if I'm in an iceberg and not on a beach with the sun beating down on me. The man's back rises and falls, telling me he's still breathing. That knowledge sends relief through me, thawing my ice-filled veins.

He's alive, not a corpse.

"Are you okay?" I ask.

It's a stupid question. This man clearly just washed onto shore from who knows where. Of course he's not okay.

His head turns at the sound of my voice and I come face to face with my ghost.

No, not me in a spiritual form. And no, not a literal ghost.

Remember the part where I said Rhett ghosted me? Yeah, he's not a ghost anymore.

ACKNOWLEDGMENTS

First and foremost, I want to thank Jesus for being with me as I penned this story. No matter how much faith I include in my books, I always want to honor Him above any other goal.

To my husband, who put up with me working long hours getting this story off the ground and onto the page (or computer screen). Without you and your steadfast devotion to our family none of this would be possible. You are the best and I can't imagine doing this life with anyone else.

To my critique partners, Dulcie and Latisha, you have been the biggest help in getting this book reader-ready. Thank you for the endless talks and string of advice you provided as I finished off this story. I seriously could not have done it without you!

And to my beta readers, Tara, Hannah, and Andie thank you for taking time out of your schedule to help me with this story. Your feedback has been crucial to making this romance the best it can be.

Of course, I need to thank my incredible editor Jennia D'Lima for all of your help in getting this story polished. I am so grateful for you and your expertise!

And to you, my dear reader, thank you for taking a chance on me and this story. I hope West and Olivia gave you a temporary yet enjoyable escape to Amber Island.

May God bless you, keep you, and shine His light on you.

xx,

Tawni

A NOTE TO READERS

Thank you for reading *When Forever Comes*.

I hope and pray all of my books encourage you in your faith journey and point you to the One who loves you eternally.

Thank you for taking a chance on me and the support you've given just by reading this novella!

God bless,

Tawni

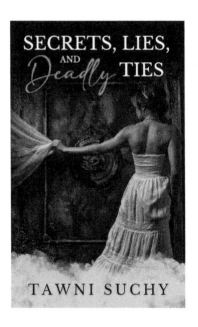

A neighbor. A locket. A lie. A secret. All leading up to one epic discovery. Tragedy has a unique way of pushing people together. But then again, so does God.

ABOUT THE AUTHOR

Tawni is a Christian wife and mother, living life to the fullest with her family. She's been writing since she could pick up a pencil which was also when God instilled a passion for storytelling into her heart.

Every story she writes contains a guaranteed happily ever after. Real life has no guarantees of happiness, but she can control her fictional worlds. Sort of. Her characters like to take her on several roller coaster rides of uncertainties, daily.

When she's not writing, she's tending to the house, playing with her kids, or on those rainy, lazy days, curled up with a good book and cup of coffee (probably with too much creamer.)

As much as she loves telling love stories between a man and woman, she hopes you discover the ultimate love story of Jesus. Her goal with each book is to show her readers the fulfillment of what having a personal, intimate relationship with Jesus Christ is like.

SIGN UP FOR TAWNI'S NEWSLETTER

Keep up to date with Tawni's latest news on book releases and events by signing up for her email list at tawnisuchy.com.

Just for signing up, you will get her free novelette *Healing Tides* a *Secrets, Lies, and Deadly Ties* prequel novella.

FOLLOW TAWNI ON SOCIAL MEDIA

@TawniSuchy   @AuthorTawniSuchy   @TawniSuchy

DID YOU ENJOY THIS BOOK?

Help others discover it by leaving a review on Goodreads and the site you purchased from!

Printed in Great Britain
by Amazon

46311388R00108